# Cat Sitter Among the Pigeons

# Cat Sitter Among the Pigeons

*A Dixie Hemingway Mystery*

## BLAIZE CLEMENT

MINOTAUR BOOKS
A Thomas Dunne Book
New York

A THOMAS DUNNE BOOK FOR MINOTAUR BOOKS.
An imprint of St. Martin's Publishing Group.

www.thomasdunnebooks.com
www.minotaurbooks.com

Library of Congress Cataloging-in-Publication Data

Clement, Blaize.
    Cat sitter among the pigeons : a Dixie Hemingway mystery / Blaize Clement.—1st ed.
        p. cm.
    "A Thomas Dunne book."
    ISBN 978-0-312-64312-6 (alk. paper)
    1. Hemingway, Dixie (Fictitious character)—Fiction. 2. Women detectives—Florida—Fiction.   3. Ex-police officers—Fiction.   4. Pet sitting—Fiction.   5. Grandfathers—Fiction. 6. Granddaughters—Fiction.   7. Swindlers and swindling—Fiction. 8. Real estate—Florida—Fiction.   9. Siesta Key (Fla.)—Fiction. I. Title.
    PS3603.L463C377 2011
    813'.6—dc22

                                                            2010037537

First Edition: January 2011

10  9  8  7  6  5  4  3  2  1

# Acknowledgments

The idea for this book was planted during a dinner conversation with Jason Jeremiah about drag racing. Thanks, Jason!

I owe a larger debt of gratitude to Pulitzer winner David Bradley, who taught me everything I know about the craft of writing. I've written several million words since David's MFA seminars at Temple University, but I still hear his voice in my head every time I write something that should be tossed out. Thanks, David.

I try to pass along everything I learned from David to the "Thursday Group"—Greg Jorgensen, Madeline Mora-Sumonte, Jane Phelan, and Linda Bailey—who meet around my dining table every week. I'm supposedly the workshop leader, but they teach me and enrich my work and my life in ways too numerous to count.

So does Marcia Markland, my patient and compassionate editor at Thomas Dunne. Thank you, Marcia! Many thanks, too, to the production department at St. Martin's Press who carefully and respectfully transform my manuscripts into finished books, to the distribution reps who see that bookstores have the books, and to all the overworked and underpaid booksellers who loyally display, recommend, and promote Dixie Hemingway.

And a huge thank you to Al Zuckerman, the über-agent at Writer's House whose wit and wisdom always astonish me.

To my family, who have endured a terrible year with grace, humor, and courage, thank you for being you.

And to readers who send me their own stories, you kept me writing through a time of grief. Thank you for your support.

If you are alone you belong entirely to yourself.
If you are accompanied by even one companion
you belong only half to yourself.

—Leonardo da Vinci

Cat Sitter
Among the
Pigeons

# 1

I read somewhere that if two quantum particles come into contact with each other—like if they happen to bump shoulders in the dairy aisle of a subatomic supermarket—they will be forever joined in some mysterious way that nobody completely understands. No matter how far apart they travel, what happens to one will affect the other. Not only that, but they will retain some eerie form of ineffable communication, passing information back and forth over time and space.

Ruby and I were a bit like those weird particles. From the moment I opened the door and saw her standing there holding her baby, we had a strong connection that neither of us particularly wanted. It was just there, an inevitable force we couldn't resist.

I met Ruby the first morning I was at her grandfather's house. Her grandfather was Mr. Stern, a name which fit him remarkably well. Slim, silver-haired, and ramrod straight, Mr. Stern had ripped his bicep playing tennis. He was not the sort of man to make a fuss about a torn muscle, but his doctor had insisted that he rest his arm in a sling until it healed. That's where I came in. Mr. Stern lived with a big orange American Shorthair named Cheddar, so he had asked me to help twice a day with cat-care things that required two hands. When he asked and I agreed, neither of us had known that Ruby was on her way with her baby. We hadn't known how much exquisite pain we'd both suffer in the following days, either. Not muscle pain, but heartache.

I'm Dixie Hemingway, no relation to you-know-who. I'm a pet sitter on Siesta Key, a semitropical barrier island off Sarasota, Florida. Until almost four years ago, I was a sworn deputy with the Sarasota County Sheriff's Department. Carried a gun. Had awards for being a crack shot. Went to crime scenes with the easy self-confidence that comes with training and experience. Had faith. Faith that I could handle anything that came along because I was solid, I was tough, I had my act together, I was on top of things. When I looked at myself in the mirror, I had calm, fearless eyes. Then my world exploded into an infinity of sharp-edged fragments and I've never had those fearless eyes again.

But on that Thursday morning in mid-September when I met Mr. Stern and Ruby for the first time, I had dragged myself out of a cold, dark pit of despair. I wasn't hollow anymore. I enjoyed life again. I had even thawed out enough to take the risk of loving again. I was actually happy. Maybe all that happiness was the reason I got careless and ended up in big trouble.

I usually make a preliminary visit to meet pet clients and provide their humans with written proof that I am both bonded and insured. The humans and I discuss my duties and fees, and we sign a contract. But since Mr. Stern had something of an emergency, my first trip to his house was also my first day on the job.

He lived on the north end of Siesta Key on one of the older streets where, during the mass hysteria that hit southwest Florida's real estate market, nice houses originally valued at two hundred thousand had sold as teardowns to be replaced with multimillion-dollar colossals.

Mr. Stern's house was a modest one-level stucco painted a deep shade of cobalt blue. In most places in the world, a cobalt house would probably seem a bit much, but on Siesta Key, where houses nestle behind a thick growth of dark greens and reds and golds, it seemed just the way God intended houses to look. It sat too close to an ostentatious wealth-flaunting house on one side, with another overblown house on the other side that had a huge untended lawn. The lawn sported a bank foreclosure sign—a not-so-subtle reminder that the real estate boom was over and that the value of anything depends on human whim, not on any intrinsic worth.

Slim as a spike of sea oats, Mr. Stern had neatly combed thin gray hair, bushy eyebrows above fierce blue eyes, and a spine so straight he didn't need to tell me he was a military veteran. He told me anyway. He also told me that he was not the kind of man to waste his time on a cat, and that the only reason he had one was that his granddaughter had left her cat at his house and now he was stuck with it. He told me this while he gently cradled Cheddar, the cat, in the crook of his good arm.

American Shorthairs are uniquely American cats.

Their ancestors came to this country along with the first settlers. They were excellent mousers—the Shorthairs, not the colonials—and they were noted for their beautiful faces and sweet dispositions. Something you can't say for sure about the first settlers.

Cheddar didn't seem the least bit offended by the way Mr. Stern talked about his disdain for cats. In fact, his lips seemed to stretch toward his ears in a secret smile, and he occasionally looked at me and blinked a few times, very slowly, sort of a cat's way of saying, *Between you and me, everything he says is hooey.*

Having made it clear that he was a no-nonsense kind of man, Mr. Stern gave me a quick tour of the house. Lots of dark leather, dark wood, paintings in heavy gilt frames, photographs scattered here and there, a book-lined library that smelled faintly of mildewed paper and pipe tobacco. Except for a sunny bedroom with flower-printed wallpaper and a net-sided crib rolled into one corner, the house was what you'd expect of a cultured gentleman who rarely had houseguests.

In the dining room, Mr. Stern opened a pair of french doors with a *ta-da!* gesture toward a large bricked courtyard. "This is our favorite place."

I could see why. Stucco walls rose a good fifteen feet high, with flowering vines spilling down their faces. Butterflies and ruby-throated hummingbirds zoomed around coral honeysuckle, Carolina jasmine, flame vine, and trumpet vine. The perimeter was a thick tangle of sweet viburnum, orange jasmine, golden dewdrop, yellow elder, firebush, and bottlebrush. A rock-lined pond held center stage, three of its sides edged with asters, milkweed, goldenrod, lobelia, and verbena, while a smooth sheet of water slid over an artfully tumbled stack of black rocks at its back. Inside the pond, several orange fish the size of a man's forearm languidly swam among water lilies and green aquatic plants.

Cheddar twisted out of Mr. Stern's hold and leaped to the terrace floor, where he made a beeline to the edge of the pond and peered at the koi with the rapt intensity of a woman gazing at a sale rack of Jimmy Choos.

I said, "This is lovely."

Mr. Stern nodded proudly. "Those gaps between the rocks make the waterfall something of a musical instrument. I can change the tone by changing the force of the water. I can make it murmur or gurgle or roar, just by turning a dial. At night, colored lights inside those openings dim or brighten on different timers. Sometimes Cheddar and I sit out here until midnight listening to the waterfall and watching the light show."

Ordinarily, when a man talks like that, he's referring to himself and a spouse or a lover. I found it both sad and sweet that Mr. Stern was a closet romantic who turned a stern face to the world but shared his sensitive side with a cat.

The churning sound of wings overhead caused us to look up at an osprey circling above us. It was eyeing the koi the same way Cheddar did, but with greater possibility of catching one. Ospreys are also called fish hawks, and they can swoop from the air and grab a fish out of water in a flash. As I watched the osprey, I saw a dark-haired young woman looking down from the upstairs window of the house next door. She turned her head as if something had distracted her, and in the next instant disappeared. Another woman appeared. The second woman was older, with the sleek, expertly cut hair of a professional businesswoman. When she saw me, her face took on a look of shock, and then changed to venomous fury. A second passed, and she jerked the drapes together and left me staring at shiny white drapery lining.

The hot air in the courtyard bounced from the bricked floor and climbed my bare legs, but a chill had moved in to sit on my shoulders. As unlikely as it seemed, the older woman's animosity had seemed personal and directed straight at me.

The osprey made another circle overhead, hovered atop the wall a moment, then extended its long stick legs for a landing. But the instant its toes touched trumpet vine, it lifted and flew away.

Mr. Stern smiled. "Those birds are smart. There's coiled razor ribbon along the top of that wall. You can't see it because it's hidden under the flowers, but that osprey sensed the danger."

The osprey's shadow had caused the koi to sense danger too. They had all disappeared under rocks and lily pads. The koi were smart to hide. In the garden paradise Mr. Stern had created, life and death teetered on a fine balance.

If I had been gifted with the ability to see into the future and know that Ruby was at that moment coming to bring danger to all of us, I would have followed the lead of the osprey and the koi. I would have hidden out of sight until the danger passed, or I would have left the place entirely and never come back. But I'm not psychic, and even though the next-door neighbor's wicked glare had been unnerving, I wasn't afraid of her.

At least not yet.

# 2

Mr. Stern scooped Cheddar up with his good arm, and I followed them inside. I opened my mouth to ask Mr. Stern if he knew the women next door, and then snapped it shut. A cardinal rule for people who work in other people's houses is to refrain from asking nosy questions about them or their neighbors.

Mr. Stern said, "Cheddar likes a coddled egg with his breakfast. Do you know how to coddle an egg?"

I said, "While I'm coddling an egg for Cheddar, how about I soft-boil one for you?" It isn't part of my job to take care of humans, but something about Mr. Stern's combination of tough irascibility and secret sensitivity reminded me of my grandfather, a man I'd loved with all my heart.

He said, "Make it three for me, and leave one in long enough to hard cook it. I'll have it later for lunch."

While I served Cheddar's coddled egg, Mr. Stern got out a plate for himself and sat down at the kitchen bar.

I said, "Would you like me to make coffee and toast to go with your egg?"

"I don't need to be babied, Ms. Hemingway." He pointed at a small flat-screen TV on the kitchen wall. "If you'll turn on the TV, I'll watch the news."

I found the remote, turned it on, and handed the remote to Mr. Stern, who was using his good hand to slap at his pockets. "Blast! I left my glasses in the library. Would you get them for me?"

I sprinted to the library to look for his glasses and found them on a campaign chest in front of a small sofa. As I snatched them up, the doorbell rang.

Mr. Stern yelled, "Would you get that? Whoever it is, tell them I don't want any."

I loped to the front door and pulled it open, ready to be polite but not welcoming.

A young woman wearing huge dark glasses and a baseball cap pulled low over blond hair stood so close to the door the suction of it opening almost pulled her inside. In skinny jeans and a loose white shirt, high heels made her an inch or two taller than me. She had a baby in a pink Onesie balanced on one forearm, a large duffel bag hanging from a shoulder, a diaper bag dangling from the other shoulder, and the hand that steadied the baby against her chest held a big pouchy leather handbag. She was looking furtively over her shoulder at a taxi pulling out of the driveway. I got the impression she was afraid somebody would see it.

Everything about her seemed oddly familiar, but I had no idea who she was.

She swung her head at me and did the same quick *I know you, no I don't* reflex that I'd done.

She said, "Who are *you*?" Without waiting for an

answer, she surged forward as if she had every right to come in.

From the kitchen, Mr. Stern yelled, "Who was it?"

The young woman called, "It's me, Granddad."

Footsteps sounded, and I could almost feel his grim disapproval before he came into the foyer with Cheddar at his heels.

His voice was frosty. "What are you doing here, Ruby?"

For a moment, the planes of her face sagged, and then she took on the hopeful look of a child who thinks she might get a different response if she asks one more time for something she's always been denied. She dropped the duffel bag on the floor and removed her dark glasses. Without them, she looked even younger than she had before, barely in her twenties. That's when I recognized her. She looked like me. Not the current me, but the me of ten years ago. She also looked desperately unhappy.

Maybe it was because I remembered what it was like to be that unhappy, or maybe it was because she reminded me of my own outgrown self, but I felt her misery like a barbed shaft hurled at my chest.

Cheddar trotted to her duffel bag and sniffed it. We all watched him as if he might do something wise that would resolve this awkward moment.

The woman said, "I don't have anyplace else to go, Granddad."

"Why don't you go to your so-called husband? Or did Zack kick you out for some other drag-race grouper?"

If he hadn't sounded so contemptuous, I would have found it amusing for him to confuse a fish with a celebrity hanger-on. But there was nothing funny about his coldness.

The woman didn't seem to notice his slip, but her hopeful look disappeared. "Please, Granddad. We won't be any trouble."

He made a sputtering sound and waved his good arm at her, which frightened the baby and made Cheddar climb atop the duffel bag and stare fixedly at him. The baby howled in that immediate, no-leading-up-to-it way that babies do, and Mr. Stern seemed shocked at the amount of noise coming from such a small form. This was something he couldn't control. The young woman looked as if she might cry too, and began to jiggle the baby as if jostling her would shut her up.

I'm a complete fool about babies. I can't be around one without wanting to cuddle it, and the sound of a baby crying makes me react like Pavlov's dog salivating at the sound of a bell. Without even asking for permission, I stepped forward and took her. I held her close so she would feel safe, murmuring softly against her bobbly head, and patted her back in the two-one heartbeat rhythm that babies listen to in the womb. I had soothed Christy that way when she was a baby, and for a moment I lost myself in the scent of innocence and the touch of tender skin brushing the side of my neck like magnolia petals. As if she recognized an experienced hand, she stopped shrieking and regarded me solemnly with wide pansy eyes.

The woman said, "Her name is Opal."

"Pretty name."

"It was my grandmother's."

A grimace of old grief twisted Mr. Stern's face. "You can stay, I guess. But nobody's going to pick up clothes you throw on the floor. And you know I like things clean."

As she reached to take the baby from me, she said, "I haven't thrown my clothes on the floor since I was thirteen, Granddad."

The baby's bottom lip puckered as if she were thinking of crying again. The woman said, "I need to change her and feed her."

Mr. Stern said, "Your old room is just like you left it."

If she found anything contradictory about Mr. Stern acting like the curmudgeon of the year one minute and then in the next minute saying he'd kept her old room unchanged, she didn't show it. Bending to grab the duffel bag, she gently edged Cheddar off it and clattered down the hall with Opal's head bobbing above her shoulder. Cheddar galloped after them.

Mr. Stern and I regarded each other with solemn faces. He said, "That's my granddaughter, Ruby. She claims she's married to a drag racer named Zack. Maybe she is, I don't know."

I said, "The granddaughter who left Cheddar with you?"

"The only granddaughter I have."

I said, "Now that she's here, I don't suppose you'll be needing me."

He snorted. "Ruby's not the kind you can depend on. I want you to keep coming."

Acutely aware of the emotions in the house, I hurried to clean Cheddar's litter box. It was in a guest bathroom across the hall from the flower-sprigged bedroom, and while I washed the box and spritzed it with a mix of water and hydrogen peroxide, I could hear Ruby's soft voice murmuring to the baby. She sounded the way I remembered sounding when Christy was a baby—the voice of a young mother absolutely besotted with her infant.

When I finished with Cheddar's litter box and headed down the hall, I glanced through the open bedroom door. Ruby had rolled the crib from the corner so it stood in front of glass sliders open to a little sunshine-filled patio. Opal and Cheddar were both in the crib. Cheddar's nose was touching Opal's chin, and Opal was laughing with the soft sound of a baby duckling. Ruby's face was naked with love. Mr. Stern had said Ruby wasn't reliable, but a woman who takes time to play with her baby and is gentle with pets goes to the top of my list of trustworthy people.

I stopped in the doorway. "That's a great crib."

It was, too. Of obvious Scandinavian design—those cold climes must create minds with a keen regard for common sense and practicality—it had a steel frame on large casters. With solid padded ends and what looked like fine fishnet stretched tightly in steel-framed drop-down sides, it combined all the advantages of a regular wooden crib without the dangers of slats or loose-fitting mesh. I was impressed that designers had made such progress in the six years since I had bought a crib.

Ruby looked up and smiled. "It was mine when I was a baby. Actually, my mother slept in it when *she* was a baby. I don't think they make them anymore." She seemed amazed at the idea of a piece of furniture holding up for three generations.

Lifting Cheddar from the crib, she set him on the floor. "Sorry, Cheddar, but it's time for Opal's nap."

Shorthairs are probably Taoists. They accept what *is*, without making a fuss about it. Shorthairs don't have legs made for high-jumping like Abyssinians or Russian Blues, so Cheddar watched Ruby raise the crib side, calculated the odds of leaping over the top rail, and yawned—the kitty equivalent of a shoulder shrug. As if sleeping under Opal's crib had been his plan all along, he oozed under it and curled himself on the floor. I'll bet cat doctors never see an American Shorthair with high blood pressure.

I wiggled my fingers at Ruby and Opal in a mock good-bye wave, and left them. I found Mr. Stern in the library. He wasn't reading or watching TV, just sitting on the sofa staring straight ahead. A grouping of framed black-and-white snapshots was on the wall behind him, all of young men in military uniform. One of them, a tall man with fierce eyes, was apparently their commanding officer. He looked like a much younger version of Mr. Stern, and for a second I wondered if he was a son. Then I noticed a framed banner bearing a red American eagle and inscribed: *The 281st Engineer Combat Battalion, 1944,* and I realized it was Mr. Stern himself. It reminded me that we can never imagine the histories of people we meet, the challenges they've faced, the losses they've known.

He said, "I guess Cheddar remembers Ruby." He sounded sad, as if he felt abandoned.

Trying to make my voice tiptoe, I said, "Cats love being with babies."

He seemed to brighten at the idea that he'd been rejected in favor of the baby instead of Ruby. As for me, a job I'd expected to be neatly delineated had become frayed around the edges by a host of complex emotions emanating from Mr. Stern and his granddaughter.

I said, "I'll be back this afternoon."

As if he'd heard a bugle call, Mr. Stern got to his feet and stood ramrod straight. He walked to the door with me, followed me outside, and watched me get in my Bronco. I gave him my most fetching smile and waved at him like somebody on a parade float. He nodded sternly, like a general acknowledging the presence of inferiors, then scurried around to the back of the car and began whirling his good arm in come-on-back motions.

I groaned. Mr. Stern was turning out to be one of those men who believes every woman with wheels needs a man to tell her how to turn them. Which sort of explained some of the tension between him and Ruby. But, okay, what the heck. It wouldn't cost me anything to let him think he was a big manly man helping a helpless female back her car out of his driveway.

Ordinarily, I would have used my rearview mirror to see if anything was behind me, but with Mr. Stern back there vigorously miming me to back straight out, I sort of felt obliged to swivel my head around and pretend to watch him. But as I looked over my shoulder I saw the young woman at the next-door house again. This time she was at a front window, and I could see her features. She was plump and plain, and something about her seemed indistinct and faded, like old sepia photographs of immigrants arriving in this country at the turn of the century. I kept looking at her until a palm tree blocked my view, and then I remembered Mr. Stern, who was in the street whirling his arm.

He was a nimble man, I'll give him that. He jumped out of the way at the right moment and back-walked along the curb, circling his arm to signal me to turn the wheel. The only problem was that he was directing me to turn in the wrong direction.

So, okay, no big deal. I pulled into the street pointed the wrong way.

I gave Mr. Stern another parade-queen wave and drove off in the wrong direction past the vacant house with the foreclosed sign. In my rearview mirror, I saw him head back toward his open front door. I also saw a long black limo pull away from the curb half a block behind me. Nothing unusual about a limo on the street. People in Siesta Key's upscale neighborhoods take limos to the airport all the time. There wasn't even anything alarming about the way the car stayed the same distance behind me. The street wasn't made for passing, so we both drove along at a steady speed.

I had intended to turn on a side street and work my way back to a main thoroughfare, but residential streets are short on the Key, and this one had no side streets. It ended in a cul de sac, where I made a U-turn. The limo driver made the same turn, and I felt a moment of camaraderie with him, both of us caught by surprise by a dead-end street. As I passed Mr. Stern's house, I looked toward the windows of the house where I'd seen the young woman, but all I saw was the glare of sunlight bouncing off glass.

That's all I could see of the windows of the limo that followed close behind me, too, because the limo's windows were tinted dark. To tell the truth, I didn't wonder about who was in that limo. My mind had drifted to

Ruby and her unhappiness, to Opal, who was one of the cutest babies I'd ever seen, and to Mr. Stern, who presented a cold face to the world but took his cat into the courtyard at night to watch light play on his waterfall.

I reminded myself that every family has its own drama, and that whatever Mr. Stern's family's drama was, it didn't involve me. No matter how much I felt Ruby's misery, no matter how cute her baby was, and no matter how much I thought Mr. Stern's stiffness was a cover-up for a soft heart, it wasn't any of my business. I was strictly a cat sitter, nothing more.

At the corner of Higel Avenue, I stopped for a break in a gaggle of cars tearing past in both directions. Then I spun right, gunned the Bronco south, and lost sight of the limo in my rearview mirror. Instead, a giant insect with long yellow antennae and a black-and-yellow-striped body hovered just behind me. The insect was atop a dark green van, which made me stop thinking about Ruby and Mr. Stern and try to decide whether the bug was an advertisement for a taxidermist or an exterminator.

Later, I would wonder how I could have been so easily distracted. My only excuse was that I'd had a man in my life—again—for about six weeks, and I still wasn't used to it.

# 3

Having a man in your life after you've lost the habit is like being hit by a persistent case of embarrassing hiccups. Jerky little blips happen in the midst of things that ought to be smooth and automatic. Like at the supermarket, you have a startled moment when you wonder if you should buy six peaches instead of three—in case he should be at your place one night and want a peach while you have one—but you don't even know if he *likes* peaches, so you stand there in front of the peaches like a total idiot asking yourself how it could be that you don't know if the man you love likes peaches. Or like when you get out of the shower, you make sure you hang your towel with the ends even in case he goes in your bathroom and judges you for hanging your towel crooked. Or like you're not sure just how the whole relationship is going to go, or how you want it to go. It's enough to make you batty, just thinking about it.

Which is what I was doing as I turned off Higel to Ocean and drove to the Village Diner where I go every morning after I've finished with all my pet-sitting duties. By that time it was close to ten o'clock. I'd been up since four, without caffeine or food, and I was ready for breakfast and a long nap.

That's my excuse. I was a woman in love, and I was hungry and tired. So when I pulled into the shelled parking area at the side of the diner, I didn't pay much attention to the black limo that purred to a stop close beside me. Like I said, Siesta Key is a prime vacation spot for well-heeled tourists, so limos are almost as numerous as egrets or herons. But when I opened the Bronco door and slid out, the limo's back door on my side opened too, which boxed me in. I did a mental shrug. As every year-round resident on the Key knows very well, some tourists are so rude and pushy that we would cheerfully toss them into the Gulf if it weren't for the fact that they keep our economy going.

Friendly as a Chamber of Commerce volunteer, I closed the Bronco door and waited for the limo's backseat occupant to get out and close the limo door so I could move forward. In the next instant, a large man in a ski mask lunged from the limo's front passenger seat and another masked man popped from the backseat. In about two nanoseconds they had my mouth covered, my limbs pinned, and me stuffed in the cavernous backseat of their car. Even in the shocked midst of it happening, while I kicked and grunted and squealed and tried to wrest myself free, part of my mind coolly appraised their expertise. These guys were pros.

The doors closed and the limo backed out of the lot and drove down Ocean at a normal speed. Both men had got into the back with me, so the driver was alone in the front. He kept his face turned forward so all I could see was the back of his head. One of the men in the back put a strip of tape over my mouth, and they had my wrists and ankles bound together before we got to Higel. As the car turned left, they pulled a black hood over my head.

Even with a hood over my head, I could tell they followed the dogleg on Higel to Siesta Drive and over the north bridge to the mainland. For a few seconds, I made angry noises. But they were a waste of energy, so I shut up and tried to pay attention to anything I could use later to identify the men. There wasn't much. The men in the back stayed silent, and so did the driver.

After the time it would take to get to the Tamiami Trail, the limo stopped, waited, and turned left. We were headed north, which led to Sarasota Bay and the marina. If they planned to put me on a boat, that would be the place to do it. North led to Sarasota's downtown streets, too, but I doubted they had shops or theaters or restaurants on their minds.

They could also turn off Tamiami onto the fixed-span bridge that leads to Bird Key, St. Armands Key, Lido Key, Longboat Key, and Anna Maria Island. Rich people live on those keys, so if some rich person had hired these goons to kidnap me, they might be taking me to the rich person's house. But I couldn't think of a single person, rich or otherwise, who would want to kidnap me.

We didn't turn off Tamiami Trail, just kept going straight ahead. My mind raced with possibilities of where we could be headed. I doubted it would be the Ringling Museum of Art, or the Ringling College of Art and Design, or the Sarasota Airport. The car kept moving and after a while I stopped trying to guess where we were going. Instead, I started wondering how long it would be before somebody realized I had been kidnapped. That was depressing because it would probably be hours.

That's one of the problems with living alone and having a weird schedule. I get up every morning at four A.M. Most days it's ten o'clock before I have contact with any being who doesn't have fur and four legs. Then I stop at the Village Diner for breakfast. Everybody knows me there, and they would notice if I didn't come in. Tanisha, the cook, always knows the minute I enter, and by the time Judy, the waitress, has my coffee on my regular table, Tanisha is already cooking my usual two eggs over easy with extra-crispy fried potatoes and a biscuit. But every now and then something comes up and I don't have breakfast there, so neither Judy nor Tanisha would think of me as a missing person if I didn't show up. They wouldn't call the cops and say they thought I'd been kidnapped.

But both of them took breaks, both of them left the diner to go home when their shifts ended. If they saw my Bronco in the parking lot, they'd wonder why it was there and I wasn't. At least they would if they recognized the Bronco as mine. I wasn't sure they would. I knew Judy and Tanisha as well as I knew anybody, but I didn't know what kind of car either of them drove. I saw them only at the diner, not driving their cars, and that's the same way they saw me. Heck, for all I knew, my Bronco could sit in that lot for two or three days without attracting any attention.

Michael, my brother, would miss me, but not for a

while. He and his life partner, Paco, live in the Gulf-side frame house where Michael and I grew up with our grandparents. I live next to them in an apartment above our four-slot carport. Michael is a fireman with the Sarasota Fire Department, so he works a twenty-four/forty-eight shift, meaning he's on duty twenty-four hours, then off forty-eight. He had gone on duty that morning at eight o'clock, so he wouldn't be home until the next morning. Paco is an undercover officer with the Sarasota County Sheriff's Department. His hours are erratic and never announced, so he might or might not come home and wonder where I was.

And then there was Guidry, a homicide detective with the Sarasota County Sheriff's Department. Guidry, with his calm gray eyes and beaky nose and a face that looks stern until you notice little white smile lines etched around his eyes. Guidry, who made my heart clatter when he was near, but who wasn't near on any regular basis because neither of us was ready yet for any kind of routine. We were more spontaneous. At least we told each other and ourselves that we were, but somehow spontaneous had added up to a lot of evenings together and a few mornings, which made us both skittish as feral cats wanting and fearing at the same time.

If Guidry called and I didn't answer, he would think I was busy grooming a cat or cleaning a litter box. If he called again and I didn't answer, he might think I was gathering information from a new client or that I was in the middle of busy traffic. But if I didn't call him back, he'd think something was wrong. Even then, he wouldn't consider that I'd been kidnapped. I mean, who gets kidnapped?

Children of wealthy parents. Heads of big multinational corporations. Big drug dealers by their rivals. Third-world politicians. Cat sitters don't get kidnapped.

The limo made a right turn, but I had lost track of where we were. All I knew was that we were quite a way north of Sarasota. After what I judged to be two or three miles, we turned left again. I could hear the whine of car tires and feel the vibration of rolling over highway joints so I guessed we had turned onto Highway 301. After several more miles, we turned right again, and went straight far enough to have crossed I-75 before we made a left, two more rights, and then a left onto a road that threw gravel onto the underside of the limo.

Another left turn, and the limo stopped. I heard electronic beeps like a control board being punched, then a sound like metal dragging on pavement, and the limo moved forward for a short distance and stopped.

One of the men pulled the hood from my head. "Okay, girlie, we're here."

I looked out the window at a smooth paved area where a jet sat in front of a gleaming white metal hangar. I don't know much about planes, but I knew this one was large for a private jet. An area of artfully planted trees and flowering shrubs separated the hangar from a rambling low-slung stucco house. The hangar looked almost like a regular freestanding garage, except it was big enough for a good-sized plane.

A tall, wide-shouldered man walked from the hangar like Donald Trump getting ready to fire somebody. He was middle-aged, gray-streaked hair combed straight back from a receding hairline, ice-blue eyes, a long face that might have been good-looking without the surly scowl.

The driver put down his electric window and grinned. "Hey, Tuck. I got her. Followed her from the old man's house."

The man leaned to look in at me, and the two masked men holding my arms tightened their grip and sort of tilted me toward the window for viewing. I did my best not to look scared when I glowered at him.

His eyes raked over my face a couple of times. His mouth twisted, and for a moment he looked frightened. Then arrogance took over again. "That's not her!"

The driver half turned to look at me. "You sure?"

"Of course I'm sure! Good God, I'm surrounded by morons and idiots!"

He fixed his cold eyes on me. "Ma'am, I want you to know I had nothing to do with this. I don't know anything about whatever these men are up to."

Turning his fury back to the driver, he said, "Take care of this, Vern!"

"Take care like—"

"No, fool! I mean fix it! With nobody getting hurt! Understand?"

Behind him, some other men had stepped from the hangar to try to get a glimpse of the wrong woman in the limo's backseat. I had a feeling I would be a lot better off with them than with Vern, so I made some more loud squealing noises, but nobody offered to take the tape off my mouth.

In a voice of hurt dignity and self-righteous demand, Vern said, "What do you want me to do with her?"

"It's your screwup, you figure it out! And don't come back here until you've got more sense!"

He went inside the hangar, sliding bay doors descended, and the interior was hidden from our view. Vern waited until the doors thudded onto the pavement with a sound of utter finality. Then, in a fury, he started the car, made a screeching K-turn, and sped through the open gate. I couldn't see them, but I was sure the gate doors closed behind us. I wondered if the man would change the code for opening the gate.

The men in the backseat released their hold on me. One of them turned his head toward me and spoke through the slit in his mask.

"I guess we made a mistake." He sounded hopeful, as if he thought I might forget the whole thing.

The other one said, "Vern, what're you going to do with her?"

I wanted to know that myself.

They hadn't replaced my hood, and in the driver's dash mirror I could see Vern's piggy little eyes darting back and forth with the effort of thinking what to do with me. I was pretty sure whatever he came up with wouldn't be anything I'd like.

His eyes met mine in the mirror. "It's just your word against ours, lady. If you tell anybody, we'll say you lied."

I nodded, trying to look humble, which took an effort. I also tried to look scared, which was no effort at all.

We retraced our route, first along the graveled one-lane road with its twists and turns, then down some streets where the lots were at least an acre, some of them with a horse or two cropping grass. I knew we were on the

outskirts of some small town, but the area wasn't familiar. It didn't seem to me that Vern had a route in mind,
but was driving aimlessly hoping for inspiration.

We finally approached an I-75 intersection where service stations and fast food places clustered in a traveler's
stop. Vern pulled into a vacant parking lot behind a Friendly's restaurant. With the motor idling, he turned to me.

"Okay, now this is what's going to happen. We're going to untie you and let you out here, and we're going to
drive away. You're going to face the other way until we're
gone, then you're going to go in Friendly's and call a cab
and you're going to go back where we got you. And you're
going to keep your mouth shut about this whole business.
*Comprende?*"

I nodded, trying to memorize his face while he talked.
He had a long upper lip that covered his top teeth. His
lowers were smoker's teeth, dark at the roots, with magenta gums. When he spoke his lower teeth were bared,
making him look like a bulldog. "If you say one word,
we'll come after you and next time it won't be for a pleasure ride. You got it?"

I nodded again. Faster.

He said, "Okay, untie her."

Untying really meant cutting through the duct tape
they'd wrapped around my wrists and ankles. Duct tape
is useless for taping ducts, but it comes in handy for kidnapping people.

I could see the men's eyes behind their ski masks.
They looked embarrassed and scared. They must have
been a lot smarter than Vern, who didn't look the least bit

embarrassed. Like every loser in the world, Vern was feeling sorry for himself.

I didn't make any sudden moves. I was docile as a Ragdoll cat. When they'd got the tape off my ankles and wrists, Vern handed me a fifty-dollar bill.

"You can use this for cab fare."

One of the other men grunted approval, and they opened the car door and moved aside so I could climb out. As soon as I was upright on the pavement, the limo door closed and the car zoomed out of the lot. Even if I'd disobeyed orders and turned around to look at the limo's tags, it was gone before I managed to force my body to stop trembling.

Gingerly, I lifted a corner of the duct tape and carefully peeled it off my mouth. It felt as if some of my lip went with it, but it didn't bleed. Holding the tape between thumb and finger, I held it away from me and walked around to the front entrance of the restaurant. A family came out before I got there, and the father held the door for me. I thanked him and walked directly to the ladies' room at the back.

As I'd hoped, a paper towel dispenser was on the wall beside the row of sinks. The towels were the smooth brown kind that are useless to dry your hands on, but perfect for preserving latent fingerprints on a strip of duct tape. I pulled a towel out, folded it loosely around the tape, and tucked it in one of the pockets of my cargo shorts. Then I leaned on the counter and shook for a while. Adrenaline does that to you. After I'd got myself more or less composed, I used the facilities, washed my hands and face, and examined my puffy lips in the mirror. Women who want lips like Angelina Jolie should forget about collagen shots and just rip some duct tape off their mouths every few days.

The only thing left to do was pull my cellphone from a pocket and call Guidry.

# 4

I didn't go into a lot of detail, just told Guidry I'd been grabbed by some guys in a limo and driven somewhere near Bradenton and put out at Friendly's.

He said, "Are you all right?"

I said I was, and he told me he'd be there in thirty minutes.

I left the ladies' room and went to sit at a table by the window. Adrenaline shakes from my harrowing experience had morphed into hunger shakes from going a lot of hours without eating. When a waitress brought a menu, I asked for immediate coffee. She not only brought me a full mug but stood by ready to give me a refill.

I winced when the hot coffee stung my lips, and the waitress looked distressed.

I said, "My lips are chapped."

She nodded, but I could tell she knew they were more than chapped. I thought about explaining that I'd lost a layer of lip skin when I ripped tape off them, but decided against it. Instead, I ordered a cheeseburger and extra-crispy fries.

The waitress must have realized I was so hungry I might start gnawing on the table, because she said, "It'll just take a few minutes. We're not real busy yet."

She topped off my coffee and scurried to turn in my order. I sat looking out the window reviewing all that had happened. Some woman had been the target of a kidnapping, but the kidnappers had been so dumb they'd nabbed me instead. It didn't take a lot of imagination to know the intended woman had been Ruby. Vern had said, "I followed her from the old man's house," which had to mean Mr. Stern's. Furthermore, even though I was a good ten years older, Ruby and I were both pale-skinned blondes, both about five-foot-three, both about a size six.

I had seen Vern's face and could identify him if I saw him again. The other two men had worn ski masks that hid their faces, but they had not worn gloves and I may have got good latents from the duct tape they'd put on my mouth.

Latent prints are only valuable if they match prints on file in IAFIS, the Integrated Automated Fingerprint Identification System maintained by the FBI. The file contains millions of prints taken from criminals, people fingerprinted in conjunction with job applications, and a large percentage of military officers and enlisted personnel, especially those taken after 2000. If the guys who'd bound and gagged me in the limo didn't have criminal records, had never worked for an employer who required fingerprints, or had not served in the U.S. military, their latents wouldn't help identify them.

While I thought about all that, the waitress brought my cheeseburger and fries. She poured another cup of coffee, hovered a moment as if she were afraid I might stuff the entire burger in my mouth at one time and choke to death, then gave me a motherly smile and left me alone.

The burger was good, with honest yellow mustard, a square of American cheese, tomato, lettuce, and a slice of onion that brought tears to my eyes just to smell it. Being as I had a man in my life and had to consider my breath, I removed the onion slice.

Mustard and salt burned my raw lips, but I finally got the hang of pulling my lips back so only my teeth touched the food. I've seen horses do that. Maybe their lips are tender too. The waitress refilled my coffee mug after I polished off the last fry. I cradled the mug with both hands and thought some more until I saw Guidry walking toward me.

Most homicide detectives wear polyester suits with drip-dry short-sleeved shirts and scuffed brown lace-ups. They wear ties either too wide or too narrow for the current style, and the buttons on their shirts are always straining against ten pounds put on since the shirt was new. Guidry wears cool unlined linen jackets with linen trousers that don't match. The jackets hang from his shoulders in a way that makes you know they were made by some Italian with an attitude. The sleeves are pushed up his bronzed forearms. The trousers are wrinkled just enough to make you think of fibers spun from grains that grew under Egyptian suns. His shirts are knit, probably of silk or some threads spun by insects I don't even know about. His bare feet are shoved into woven leather sandals. Good leather, not that cheap cardboard-like stuff.

He does not wear ties, but lets his shirts lie open at his throat. His throat has a little hollow between the bones that my lips fit into perfectly. It smells of clean skin and honesty.

He looked calm as ever, but the lines around his lips seemed deeper and his gray eyes were stormy. He slid into a chair opposite me and studied my face.

He said, "Are you really okay?"

I nodded. "They put a hood over my head and wrapped duct tape around my wrists and ankles, but they didn't hurt me."

"Your mouth is swollen."

"They put tape on my mouth too. I saved the tape for prints."

"You know who they were?"

"There were three of them. The driver's name was Vern. Caucasian, about forty, broad shoulders. I didn't see him standing up, but he looked tall in the seat. The other two were also Caucasian, medium height, medium weight, wore ski masks. I heard one of them speak, but there wasn't anything distinctive about his voice."

"What'd he say?"

"He said, 'I guess we made a mistake.'"

Guidry raised a *no-shit!* eyebrow.

I said, "They meant to kidnap a different woman."

"What different woman?"

"I'm pretty sure they thought I was a woman named Ruby. She's the granddaughter of a man who has a cat I'm helping him with. He tore his bicep muscle. The man, not the cat. The cat is a big orange Shorthair named Cheddar. The man's name is Mr. Stern."

Guidry's gray eyes took on the bleak look he gets when I talk about animals.

I said, "They took me to a man named Tuck. He has a big hangar next to his house, with a landing strip for a private jet. Tuck walked out to the limo and I think he was expecting me. Vern said, 'I got her,' but when Tuck saw my face he said, 'That's not her!' He was mad at Vern, and told him to take care of me without anybody getting hurt. He apologized to me, said he hadn't had anything to do with it and didn't know anything about it, but I think he did."

"Where were you when they grabbed you?"

"The Village Diner parking lot. They drove in and parked right beside me."

"They'd been following you?"

I hesitated, embarrassed to admit I hadn't been paying attention. "A limo like theirs was behind me earlier, but traffic got between us on Higel. I didn't see them back there when I turned on Ocean, but they must have been."

"Where were you earlier, when you saw them behind you?"

I told him where Mr. Stern lived. "The limo was a couple of houses down the street when I left Mr. Stern. It pulled behind me and stayed on my tail until I turned on Higel. Vern told Tuck he'd followed me from 'the old man's house,' as if they both knew who 'the old man' was. I think he meant Mr. Stern's house."

I touched my sore lips. "Ruby doesn't live there, but she has a bedroom with a crib in it so she must have spent a lot of time with Mr. Stern. She's been gone someplace, but she came back this morning while I was there. Ruby's at least ten years younger than me, but we look a lot alike.

She has an adorable baby named Opal. She's about four months old."

Guidry got the same expression he got when I talked about pets. "You know Ruby's last name?"

I shook my head. "Mr. Stern said she might or might not be married to a drag racer named Zack. He seemed to think Ruby might have lied about being married to him."

"Zack Carlyle?"

The way he said the name made it sound as if Zack Carlyle was somebody famous. I guess he could tell from my blank face that I'd never heard the name before.

He said, "This guy Tuck, was his place east of Seventy-five?"

I nodded. "It's that super wealthy area where all the homes have private landing strips and hangars."

"Tuck is probably Kantor Tucker. Richer than God, flies his own big jet, has lots of important contacts."

I'd never heard of him, either. Once again, I realized that I was ignorant about a lot more things than I was smart about. I hate when that happens.

Guidry looked down at me and quirked the corner of his mouth. "So Vern and his boys drove you here and let you out?"

"Vern gave me fifty dollars for cab fare."

"Vern's all heart."

"I ate a cheeseburger and I'm going to use Vern's fifty to pay for it. You want one?"

He grinned and refused, his smile a white flash that never fails to make my toes tingle.

With tax, my hamburger and coffee were a little over ten dollars. I left the rest of the fifty for the waitress.

# 5

On the way back to Sarasota, Guidry and I were both quiet. I don't know what Guidry was thinking, but I was thinking that once my kidnapping was reported, it would be a matter of public record. Which meant that local reporters who troll police reports for news would see it. Which meant that my private life would be displayed for the world to see. Again.

In my mind, I played out two options and their consequences. I could report that I'd been kidnapped and go through the law-enforcement process of identifying Vern and his cohorts, or I could keep quiet about the whole thing.

*If* I could identify Vern from mug shots, and *if* the latent prints on the tape weren't too smudged, and *if* IAFIS had matching prints in their files, the cops could identify the man who had taped my mouth. Those were important *if*s, because the tape was the only proof I had that the kidnapping had actually happened. If the tape had no usable latent prints, it wouldn't be proof at all.

If Vern and his goons were brought to trial, I knew how it would go. Their lawyers would argue the kidnapping hadn't happened, that even if it had, I hadn't been hurt, hadn't been taken across state lines, hadn't been raped, hadn't been threatened with a gun or a knife. They would say it wasn't really kidnapping because nobody had made ransom demands. They'd claim they had simply taken me for a short ride as a harmless prank. They'd pull self-righteous faces and claim that as soon as Vern had realized it wasn't funny to me, he'd let me go with money for cab fare.

A smart lawyer would make me look like a whining neurotic who took herself far too seriously. Even if a jury believed I'd been taken by force, the penalty probably wouldn't be very severe.

And then there was wealthy Kantor Tucker, who would surely deny that he'd ever seen me. He was a man in the public eye, and if I said I'd been kidnapped and taken to him, the media would have a field day playing with the fact that Vern had grabbed me for Tucker and Tucker had refused me. On top of everything else, I would look like a kidnap rejectee.

I said, "I'm not going to report it."

Guidry gave me a quick sideways look. "You have to put an end to that fear, Dixie."

"Easy for you to say. You aren't the one who got pilloried by the press."

I sounded bitter and self-pitying, which bothered me more than memories of seeing myself on TV lunging at a woman reporter at Todd and Christy's funeral. My face had been twisted in a murderous rage, and if Michael and

Paco hadn't grabbed me, I probably would have choked the woman right there on camera. She had stuck a mike in my face and asked me how it felt to lose my husband and child in such a senseless way, and I'd gone mad-dog crazy. The next time I'd made the news was when I killed a man. That time I was a heroine, but the slimy feeling I'd had when I saw my name in headlines had been as bad as the first time I'd seen it. I didn't want to see it again. Didn't want to read: PET SITTER KIDNAPPED.

But I knew what Guidry was thinking: my reason for keeping quiet about a crime shouldn't be solely to avoid publicity. If I didn't report it, criminals would have gotten away with treating a woman like an object to be carted around at their whim. They might feel so invincible they'd commit some other crime against some other woman, and next time they might not stop at nabbing her off the street.

With a defensive whine to my voice, I said, "If I thought bringing charges against them would send them to jail or get them a hefty fine, it would be different."

Guidry didn't respond, but I could see by the way his lips firmed that he didn't believe either of those penalties would happen. One of the paradoxes of living in a democracy governed by laws is that laws sometimes work in favor of law-breakers more than law-keepers. I don't like that, but I also wouldn't like living in a country where some dictator made the rules.

We rode awhile longer in silence, then Guidry said the words I should have expected, but hadn't. "Dixie, I'm a sworn officer of the law. I have to report any crime I have knowledge of."

For a moment, I felt betrayed, even though I knew he was right. For another moment, I wished I'd used Vern's money to pay a cab and kept the whole incident a secret. But I knew that would have been wrong, too. I didn't want my relationship with Guidry to include secrets. Secrets may start out as little cracks between two people, but they end up as chasms a mile wide.

I scooched forward on the seat and dug my Keds into the floor, knowing that Guidry would drive me straight to the sheriff's office on Ringling Boulevard, where I would look at mug shots of known criminals who matched Vern's description.

That's exactly what he did, too. The problem with people with ethics is that they have ethics all the time, even when it's inconvenient. So I reported the crime, handed over the duct tape I'd peeled from my lips, and spent two hours looking at mug shots that did not include any face I recognized as Vern's.

When the investigators were done with me, Guidry drove me to my Bronco in the Village Diner's parking lot. After he parked and turned off the engine, he turned in his seat and slid an arm around my shoulder.

"That wasn't so bad, was it?"

"That wasn't what I dread, and you know it."

He rubbed his thumb against my shoulder bone. "Look, it's bad enough that you may get some embarrassing mention in the press. But if it happens, deal with it then. You're reacting to something that hasn't even happened yet."

At times like that I always wish I chewed bubble gum. If I did, I could blow a big round balloon and pop it right in somebody's face every time they were right and I was wrong. Since I couldn't do that, I just stuck out my lower lip a little bit like a two-year-old.

Guidry patted my shoulder like I was a puppy. "I'll follow you home. Check out your apartment, make sure everything is okay."

I gave him a cool look. "This morning, a man directed me when I backed out of his driveway. It was a straight driveway."

"Are you saying I'm a control freak like him?"

I leaned forward and kissed his cheek. "I'm saying I'm a big girl, and I don't need you to follow me home. At least not to check out my apartment."

He took a deep breath. "If you see that limo again, get the tag number."

"I will."

"And be careful when you go home."

"I will."

He pulled me close and kissed my sore lips so lightly it was like being touched by a butterfly's wing. But a good kisser can put a lot of passion into the tenderest of kisses, and Guidry is an excellent kisser. Oh, yes, he is. So good that I may have staggered a little bit when I slid out of his car and got into my own. I hoped he didn't notice. I mean, I have my pride.

He waited until I started the Bronco and drove out of the lot, then followed me as far as Midnight Pass Road where I turned south. He tooted his horn goodbye and turned north. I drove home with a goofy grin on my face. Somehow the kiss had made the morning's unpleasantness not seem so bad anymore.

I sure as heck didn't look forward to the media finding out about it. I didn't feel optimistic about Vern and his buddies being punished for kidnapping me, either. But it had been cowardly of me to even consider keeping it a secret and I was glad Guidry had pushed for what was right.

Furthermore, even though I hadn't seen Vern's face in the mug shots, I knew it would take deputies handling the investigation about two nanoseconds to find out who Vern was. I had no idea what would happen after that, but I knew at least two deputies—Guidry and Paco—who would take an extremely personal interest in the investigation.

Guidry wouldn't be part of the investigating team because he was homicide, and Paco wouldn't be part of it because he did drug busts and undercover surveillance, but they would both pay close attention. Female logic made me see that kind of male protectiveness as a good thing, not at all like Guidry's offer to follow me home or like Mr. Stern directing me out of a straight-shot driveway.

Like a hunting dog finding all kinds of tantalizing scents in the woods to explore, I let my mind trot down several trails. Vern hadn't struck me as the kind of man who was trusted to make independent decisions, so I doubted he had just happened to see me leaving Mr. Stern's house and decided to grab me. If I was right, somebody had ordered him to take me to Kantor Tucker. But who? Tucker had no way of knowing I was at Mr. Stern's, so it wouldn't have been him. And certainly Mr. Stern wouldn't have called Vern and told him to follow me and kidnap me.

I thought about the woman who had looked down at me with such venom from her second-story window. Her face had held outraged anger, as if she'd had personal animosity toward me. Could she have mistaken me for Ruby and called Vern to grab me? If so, why had she wanted Ruby kidnapped and taken to Kantor Tucker?

The biggest question of all, of course, was what would have happened to Ruby if Vern had got her instead of me.

Whatever the answer was to those questions, I had to let Ruby know that somebody meant her harm. And as soon as I did, I would be stepping into somebody else's life, something I had vowed not to do again. But sometimes you have to speak up, especially if it might be a life-or-death situation for another person. In this case, I had a strong feeling that it definitely was a matter of life or death.

# 6

Sunlight, humidity, and sandy sea breezes have softened all the hard edges on Siesta Key. Petals of hibiscus blossoms are indistinct at their edges, palm fronds are faintly fringed at their borders. Even the thorns on the bougainvillea have a vagueness at their tips as if they might decide to turn soft if the idea pleased them. All over the island the lines are sinuous, undulating, ambiguous.

The Key is eight miles long, north to south. We are bordered on the west by the Gulf of Mexico and on the east by Roberts Bay and Little Sarasota Bay. We have some of the finest beaches in the world, some of the wealthiest part-time celebrity residents in the world, and a steady current of sun-dazzled tourists. We also have every shorebird and songbird you can think of, manatees, dolphins, the occasional shark, and semitropical foliage that would smother us in a minute if we didn't keep it trimmed back. The Key is where I was born and where I will die. If I moved someplace else, I wouldn't be me.

Midnight Pass Road cuts a north–south line through the center, with short meandering residential lanes leading east and west. Siesta Beach and Crescent Beach, where the sand is like cool powdered sugar, are on the western Gulf side. Turtle Beach, where the sand is more gray and dense and is a favorite place for people who like to collect shells, is at the extreme southern end.

I live on the south end of the Key on the Gulf side, at the end of a twisty shelled road lined with oaks, pines, palms, and sea grape. Colonies of parakeets live in the treetops, squirrels make their homes in the trunks, and rabbits nibble at the vegetation on the ground. Every time I make the final curve in the lane and see the sun-glittered sea lapping at the shoreline, my heart does a little jig of gratitude for my grandfather's good fortune to stumble on our little curved piece of beachfront paradise back in the thirties.

He had been traveling through Florida on business, land in Florida was dirt cheap, and he had known then and there that he'd found his true home. He and my grandmother bought a two-story frame house from the Sears, Roebuck catalogue, set it facing the Gulf, and raised my mother there. Later, after my father had died and my mother had left us, my brother and I went to live in that house with our grandparents. I was nine, Michael was eleven. When our grandparents died, Michael and his partner, Paco, moved into the house. Almost four years ago, after my husband and little girl were killed, I came back to live in the apartment above the carport. The house and the apartment are like a lot of native Floridians, old and weathered, but strong and sheltering.

I parked in my slot in the carport and stepped into the

brooding torpor peculiar to early afternoon on the coast. During those hours, when the lasering sun seems to draw closer, the sea's hot breath wilts everything in its path and seabirds and songbirds desert the beach for siestas. Even rippling waves lower their heads to conserve energy.

As I went up the stairs to my apartment, I used my remote to raise metal hurricane shutters that cover the entry doors. The shutters were halfway to their soffit when I got to the top of the steps, and I could see Ella Fitzgerald peering at me through the glass in the french doors. Ella is a true calico Persian mix, meaning she's mostly Persian and her coat has distinct blocks of vivid red, white, and black. Ella got her name from the little scatting noises she makes. She had originally been a gift to me, but in no time she had given her heart to Michael and Paco. A lot of females do that when they meet Michael and Paco. Fat lot of good it does them.

A long covered porch runs the length of my apartment. It has two ceiling fans, a hammock strung in one corner, and a glass-topped iron table and two chairs. The roof provides shade, but at noon the porch is almost as hot as the rest of the Key. I unlocked the door and stepped into air-conditioned coolness.

Ella twined around my ankles and said, "Thrripp!"

I picked her up and kissed her nose. "I'm sorry I'm late. I got kidnapped."

She looked deeply into my eyes and blinked slowly. She did it twice, which in cat language means *I love you.* I blinked back at her in the same language, even though I knew she would drop me like a hot lizard if she had to choose between me and Michael or Paco.

Ella officially lives with them, but we don't like to leave her alone any more than we have to, so whichever man is last to leave the house in the morning brings Ella to my apartment. When I come home, she and I take a siesta together and she sits with me while I do clerical duties that go along with a pet-sitting business.

My entire apartment is the same neutral creamy white that my grandfather put on it when he built it for visiting relatives. I guess it seems spartan to other people, but it suits me just fine. The living room has a love seat and club chair covered in dark green linen printed with red and yellow flowers. My grandmother bought the set for her little personal parlor that she'd created with the intention of finding privacy from the rest of us, but I don't think she ever sat on it much. There's also a coffee table and a couple of side tables with lamps. No pictures on the walls. No houseplants. No doodads sitting around.

A one-person bar separates the living room from the kitchen, which is about the size of the postage stamps of some developing countries. A window over the sink looks out at the driveway and its trees.

My bedroom is to the left of the living room. It's only big enough for a single bed pushed against the wall, a nightstand, and a dresser. Photos of Todd and Christy sit on the dresser, and I always pause to touch them when I come home. Todd was thirty-two when he was killed, Christy was three.

I grieved so deeply when they died that I will never be the same person again. Grief is about the loss of yourself as much as the loss of a loved one. The person you were when you were with the other is gone forever. You'll never be exactly the same with anybody else, laugh at the same jokes, share the same private memories. The special facet of yourself they brought out is dimmed or erased forever. I have created a new self without Todd and Christy, but they continue to live somewhere in my mind, healthy and laughing. I suppose they always will.

A door in the bedroom leads to a hall where a stacked washer and dryer sit in an alcove. To the left of the alcove is a small bathroom. To the right is a large closet big enough for clothes on one side and a desk on the other. I take care of my pet-sitting business at the desk, so half of my closet—about thirty-six square feet—qualifies as an office for tax-reporting purposes. I'll bet that gives some IRS guy a big laugh.

I put Ella on my bed, and on the way to the bathroom peeled off my clothes, including my Keds, and put them in the washer. In the shower, I shampooed my hair and stood a long time under a warm spray in case Vern and his goons had shed any of their skin cells on me. Just the thought made my skin quiver.

Out of the shower, I patted myself mostly dry, pulled a comb through my wet hair, brushed my teeth, smoothed on some conditioner, and slicked some Vaseline on my sore lips. My mouth looked like the pouting lips of weird dark-water fish I've seen on the Discovery Channel. Naked, I padded to the hall, added my damp towel to the clothes in the washer, threw in detergent, and turned the thing on. Then I climbed into bed and let the washer's sounds of filling and sloshing and spinning make a homely symphony while Ella and I slept.

When I woke, the kidnapping incident seemed like a

dream. Not a nice dream, but not a nightmare either. On a scale of one to ten, compared to the worst experiences of my life, it didn't even rate a two or three. More like a one-plus. Except for the niggling question of what the connection was between Vern and Tucker and Ruby, I was totally over it.

To convince myself of how over it I was, I focused on my mundane routine as if it were a meditation practice. I made myself a cup of tea, then I flipped the switch on my CD player and listened to Tommy Castro doing "Let's Give Love a Try" while I tossed wet laundry into the dryer and got dressed. With Ella sitting on my desk, I entered morning visits in my client record. The music changed to Eric Clapton's blues. Ella flexed the tip of her tail to the beat. After I finished the office work, I took Ella down to the redwood deck between the house and my apartment, put her on a table my grandfather built, and groomed her. I had just finished going over her with a brush to make her coat shine when Guidry's dark Blazer rounded the curve of the lane. He parked beside the carport and walked to the deck, where he and Ella gave each other appraising looks.

I was all set to kiss him, or at least hug, but he had a removed look that told me he was having some kind of internal debate.

He said, "Ah . . . I have to tell you something. I would have told you earlier, but it didn't seem like the right time."

I felt a prickle of alarm. When somebody is reluctant to tell you something, it's usually bad news.

I said, "Is Michael okay? Paco?"

He looked surprised. "It's not anything like that."

I felt myself blush. "Sorry, I guess I'm still jumpy."

He colored a bit himself, and seemed sorry he'd said anything. When he spoke, I suspected he'd dredged up something to say that didn't have anything to do with what he'd originally intended to say.

"I checked the records. Ruby and Zack Carlyle were married eighteen months ago."

The air seemed to have thinned around us. One of the advantages of having an alcoholic mother is that children get a sixth sense that tells them when they're being lied to. Guidry wasn't exactly lying, but I didn't believe he had come to talk about Ruby's marriage. He'd had some other intent and then changed his mind.

That's one of the problems inherent in a new relationship, when both people have scars from former unions. You have to step carefully, be constantly mindful of where you stand and where you want to go.

Taking the safe route, I pretended to believe Guidry had truly come only to tell me that Ruby was married to a race car driver. "So they're really married."

"There are no records of a divorce."

"Any other kinds of records?"

"He's clean, but the investigators will want to talk to Zack about your kidnapping."

From the grim sound of his voice, I got the impression that Guidry took my kidnapping personally, as if it had been a gauntlet thrown down for him. I suppose it's a guy thing to feel that everything that happens to your woman might be a challenge to your masculinity.

I said, "I don't think Zack had anything to do with me being kidnapped."

"You can't be sure of that. The guy who kidnapped you thought you were Zack's wife."

Well, yeah, there was that.

Ella turned her head and looked at me with something of alarm in her eyes.

All of a sudden the memory of Vern's angry eyes came barreling at me, and I felt my fear again, remembered how my heart had pounded, remembered how scary it had been to have my head covered and my mouth taped shut, how frightened I'd been when I didn't know what was going on, who my captors were, what they planned for me. Even if Zack Carlyle's involvement was totally tangential, he was involved through Ruby, and his part couldn't be ignored.

I must have zoned out for a moment remembering the morning, because Guidry caught my attention with a light tap on my shoulder. He leaned to kiss my cheek and said, "See you later."

Ella and I watched him walk to his Blazer and drive away. I don't know what Ella was thinking, but I was wondering *Later like when?*

That's the thing about men. They're not specific. They come to your house intending to tell you something important, but then they change their mind and talk about something else. They leave you dangling with indefinite words like *later* and *sometime* and *see you*. They really are the most exasperating other sex in the world.

# 7

When it was time to make afternoon pet rounds, I put Ella in Michael's kitchen and headed for my first stop. Always, mornings and afternoons, that's at Tom Hale's condo in the Sea Breeze on Midnight Pass Road. Tom's a CPA who has been in a wheelchair since a wall of wooden doors fell on him at a home improvement store, so I go twice a day and run with his greyhound, Billy Elliot. In exchange, Tom handles my taxes and anything having to do with money.

I parked in the big lot in front of the condo and took the elevator to Tom's place. He and Billy Elliot were watching *Oprah* on TV. It must have been a show about physical fitness because Oprah was watching a man on a metal contraption hoist himself upwards, like chinning. His arms were shaking from the strain, but he kept doing it, over and over. Except for his middle-aged body, he looked like a kid showing off for a girl. Oprah looked slightly bored. She's probably used to men showing off for her.

Tom switched off the TV and watched me snap Billy's

leash on his collar. Tom has a mop of curly black hair and wears round Harry Potter glasses. He's like a cute poodle you want to pet on the head.

He said, "How're you holding up in the heat?"

I would have told him that the heat wasn't as bad as being kidnapped, but Billy Elliot whuffed to remind me that I was there to run with him, not to chat with Tom, so I led Billy out to the elevator in the hall. Downstairs, we went out to the parking lot where cars park in an oval around a central green spot. The track between parking spaces and the center makes a perfect running track for me and Billy. Like the kind of track I imagined all race cars sped around on.

Contrary to their reputation, some greyhounds don't enjoy running at all. They'd rather sit and watch TV. But not Billy Elliot. Billy Elliot likes running better than anything in the world. He doesn't run because he's a greyhound, he runs because he's like those people who get up early every morning and run two or three miles just for the fun of it. I don't understand those people, but I'm sure Billy does.

After he'd peed on every tree trunk he thought needed peeing on, Billy led me onto the track and we set off. Billy is considerate. He always begins slowly so my muscles can get warmed up before he really takes off. But about halfway around the track, he speeds up. By the time we've made two rounds of the track I feel like a lab rat trying to stay upright on a moving conveyor set too fast. At the condo entrance, I pulled Billy to a stop and leaned over and panted with my hands on my knees. A grandmotherly woman came from the building carrying a white

Lhasa Apso with Cindy Lou Who hair tied with a pink ribbon on top of its head.

The woman stopped. "Are you all right?"

I wheezed, "Just out of breath."

She walked on toward her parked car while the Lhasa looked over her shoulder at me. Before she got into her car, the woman called, "Awfully hot to be running."

I nodded and flapped my hand to say thanks for the tip, while Billy pranced around me, grinning. When we went inside and got into the mirrored elevator, my face was still beet red. Billy was still grinning and wagging his tail in doggy joy.

In Tom's apartment, I went in the kitchen where he was at the table typing on a slim laptop computer. Personally, I'm not a computer person. I'm probably the only living person in the western hemisphere without a Web site or an e-mail address. My life is complicated enough without adding all that electronic crap to it, so I don't blog, Twitter, Facebook, YouTube, Google, or text-message. But every now and then, when I want to take advantage of the availability of instant information, I impose on friends who are computer savvy. People like Tom.

I got myself a glass, filled it with water from the tap, and rested my back against the countertop edge while I drank it.

I said, "If I gave you an address, could you find the person who lives there?"

With his fingertips poised above the keys, he looked at me over the top of his glasses. "What's the address?"

I gave him the house next door to Mr. Stern, the one

where I'd seen two women looking out the window. In about two nanoseconds, he had the owner's name.

"Myra Kreigle."

I went still, with the same kind of *something's-not-right* feeling that comes just before you realize you've stepped into thong bikinis wrong so the crotch part is riding on your hip. I had asked about the address because I wanted to know who had looked down at me with such fury from the house next door to Mr. Stern. Now that I knew she was Myra Kreigle, the way she'd looked at me seemed even more peculiar.

Tom said, "You know who Myra Kreigle is?"

"Sure, the big flipper."

In Sarasota, *big flippers* once meant the appendages loggerhead turtles use to propel themselves onto the beach every year to lay eggs. Now it means somebody who fraudulently drove up real estate prices and fueled southwest Florida's economic meltdown.

Tom said, "Worse than that. Myra Kreigle was a big flipper with an REIT Ponzi scheme."

I vaguely remembered skimming over newspaper headlines when Myra Kreigle was indicted for fraud in connection to her real estate investment company. A vivacious, attractive woman in her fifties, Myra's photo had usually been in the paper in connection to her investment seminars or because she'd donated money to a charity or an arts association. I had been surprised to learn of her dark side, but since I didn't travel in Myra's social circle, she had only been a name to me, not a real person.

Tom said, "She's used up all her trial postponements.

They've already selected the jury, and her hearing starts
Monday."

I hadn't even known a trial date had been set. I wondered if the young woman I'd seen at Myra's window was
her daughter. If she was, having a notorious liar for a
mother would explain why she looked so unhappy. My
mother had been a liar too, so I could relate.

I said, "Can you tell me in twenty words or less exactly
what Myra did?"

"It'll take more than twenty words, but I'll condense
it as much as possible. You know how flipping works,
right?"

"Somebody buys a house at its real value, then gets an
appraiser to inflate the value. He does a bogus sale to an
accomplice at that inflated price. The accomplice gets a
mortgage, a banker who knows what's going on lends
the money and gets a bonus, and the accomplice either
passes the money he borrowed to the seller or they split
it. Then the buyer walks away and lets the house be foreclosed on."

"That's how small flippers worked. Big flippers formed
a bunch of post-office-box companies or limited partner-
ships and sold the same property back and forth between
them with ever bigger appraisals, larger mortgages, more
profits. Myra Kreigle bought and sold hundreds of prop-
erties that way. That in itself was a crime, but Myra had
formed a real estate investment trust, otherwise known as
an REIT, through which she suckered investors by telling
them they would get double-digit returns if they gave her
money to invest in real estate. About two thousand people
fell for that, but it was a scam."

Any time people talk about big money, I always feel like my eyeballs are rotating. Maybe they really were, because Tom grinned and began to speak more slowly.

"A Ponzi scheme is when a lot of people invest in something too good to be true. The con pays the first investors from the money the later investors put in, so word spreads and more people rush to get in on a good deal. As long as new investors are pouring in money, it works. There's enough money to pay off people who ask for their profits, and the con running the scheme can live high on the hog on other people's money."

"So Myra never really invested in real estate?"

"Oh, she bought some mortgages, but most of them were high risk, and none of them paid back what she was promising her investors. The fraud was in sending her investors false monthly reports showing huge profits she claimed she'd made for them by brilliant real estate trades. Most people let their profits ride, but if somebody wanted to collect, she paid them from the investment money. She took in nearly two hundred million dollars that way. Her investors will never get their money back. I imagine most of it is socked away in offshore banks."

"I don't understand how she got away with it for so long."

He rolled his eyes. "If pigeons are getting fed, they aren't picky about who's feeding them."

I nodded, but I still didn't see how intelligent people could be fooled so easily.

Tom said, "Ponzi schemes are called *affinity* crimes because the criminal preys on his own people. Fundamentalists hoodwink fundamentalists, New Agers manipulate

New Agers, Catholics scam fellow Catholics. Myra went after her own kind."

Myra's own kind were the cream of Sarasota's society, the smart set who ordered three-hundred-dollar wine when they lunched at Zoria's. Smugly confident, they were the beautiful people who traveled the world, went to all the classy parties, had their photos in the society pages. Myra had smiled, beguiled, sucked the fat right off their sucker bones, and left them gasping for air like stranded fish. When they went down, they took with them all the little people who had cleaned their houses, landscaped their lawns, taught their children, and sold them goods.

Tom continued to tap keys on his computer and peer at his screen. Some people can multitask like that. Personally, I have difficulty talking and walking at the same time. His fingers raised from the keyboard and he leaned toward the screen to read something he'd pulled up. He wrinkled his lips like he'd bit into moldy cheese, and closed his laptop.

"It'll take a decade before our economy gets back to normal. Myra Kreigle should be in jail now, and if that Tucker guy hadn't put up a two-million-dollar bond for her, she would be."

The short hairs on the back of my neck stood up.

"Kantor Tucker?"

"That's the one. Everybody else thought she was a flight risk, but Tucker is a close friend and put up the money. He can't protect her forever, though. State investigators have a solid case against her. Several counts of securities fraud, mail fraud, wire fraud, and money laundering fraud. Unless something happens to make the case fall through, she'll serve several years in a white-collar-crime prison."

I finished off the glass of water and filled it again. "Some guys kidnapped me this morning and took me to Kantor Tucker."

Now I had Tom's complete attention. "Somebody *kidnapped* you?"

"They grabbed me outside the Village Diner and drove me east of Seventy-five where Tucker has a place. Big spread with a landing strip and a hangar beside his house. The guys who took me to him thought I was somebody else. When they found out I wasn't who they thought I was, they took me to a Friendly's and put me out. I called Guidry and he came and got me. I reported it. I don't want the publicity, and I can't prove they did it, but Guidry made me report it."

"Good God, Dixie."

"I know. I looked at mug shots at the sheriff's office but I didn't see the driver of the limo. His name is Vern."

"That's all you've got? The guy's first name?"

"They put tape on my mouth, and I saved the tape. It may have latent prints on it. I gave it to the investigators."

"Is that why your mouth is puffy?"

"Is it still puffy?"

"I thought maybe you and Guidry had been playing rough kissy-face."

I took another drink of water. "Some of my lip skin stayed on the tape when I ripped it off."

His hand rose to his own lips as if he needed to confirm they were in one piece. "Who did they think you were?"

I shrugged. "They didn't say anybody's name." Strictly speaking, that was true.

"Do you think grabbing you had something to do with Myra Kreigle?"

"Not really. Probably just a coincidence that the limo was in front of her house when I left the house next door."

I tried to sound convincing, but Tom knows me well enough to know when I'm not being totally honest.

I got busy emptying my water glass and putting it in the dishwasher. When I left, Tom and Billy Elliot watched me leave with identical wrinkled brows. Billy Elliot was probably pondering how long it would be before he and I ran again. Tom was probably wondering what Myra Kreigle had to do with me being kidnapped.

So was I.

# 8

Myra Kreigle and her kind weren't the first real estate swindlers in Sarasota's history. As Sarasota became fashionable during the 1920s, the town was flooded with land speculators who sent property values skyrocketing. Fortune hunters razed orange groves for subdivisions, but left without completing them. People bought property in the morning and sold it for a profit that same afternoon. But in September of 1926, a destructive hurricane ended the real estate boom. The Great Depression struck next, when businesses went broke and tourism slowed to a trickle.

By the 1950s, land was selling again, but not to speculators. In a period of sane and responsible growth, shopping centers, housing developments, schools, churches, and condos went up, all intended for families and retirees seeking a pleasant life. Sarasota would not see another overwrought speculator-fueled boom until Myra Kreigle and her cohorts saw the opportunity to cheat people through fraudulent real estate deals. When I thought of what my grandfather would have had to say about Myra Kreigle, I had to grin. He was a man who could be persuaded to suffer fools, but not thieves. More than likely, he and Mr. Stern would have enjoyed each other's company.

I pulled into Mr. Stern's driveway that afternoon around the time retirees in Florida start crowding into restaurants for the Early Bird Specials. As I started up the walk, a three-woman cleaning crew came out the front door lugging a vacuum cleaner and a plastic basket holding supplies. The woman carrying the vacuum was young and obese and weeping. The other two were thin and older, and were murmuring comforting words to her. They passed by me with barely a look. I suspected that Mr. Stern had said something that had hurt the crying woman's feelings.

Ruby opened the door with Opal balanced on her forearm. Mr. Stern stood behind her with Cheddar cradled in his good arm. They seemed to be in the middle of an argument.

Mr. Stern said, "If American GIs had stopped work every time they got upset, we'd all be speaking German."

Ruby said, "She lost a baby last month. She got upset when she saw Opal."

As if she understood what her mother had said, Opal's bottom lip trembled and she wept for a minute. Ruby jiggled her and Opal hushed and closed her eyes. She probably thought it was the only way to stop being jiggled. I forced my arms to stay at my sides and not reach for her.

Mr. Stern said, "How do you know she lost a baby? Did she waste more time telling you about it?"

"I'll finish the vacuuming, Granddad."

Mr. Stern snorted and stalked off toward the kitchen. Exasperated, Ruby rolled her eyes and walked toward her bedroom, while Opal's round eyes stared at me over Ruby's shoulder.

I followed Mr. Stern to the kitchen where he took a seat at the bar and watched me shake dry food into Cheddar's bowl.

He said, "Cheddar takes a chicken liver in his dinner. There's a tub of them in the refrigerator. Don't heat it. Just put it on top of the food."

The contrast between the consideration Mr. Stern showed Cheddar and the lack of consideration he showed human beings was striking, but not shocking. Pets bring out the hidden goodness in the most hardened hearts, even if it's only in tiny amounts.

I dropped a chicken liver in Cheddar's dish, and Mr. Stern gave a nod of approval. Cheddar jumped on the food and gobbled it up while I washed his water bowl and filled it with fresh water. Mr. Stern's gaze drifted toward a wine rack at the end of the kitchen counter.

I said, "Hard to use a corkscrew with one hand. Shall I open a bottle of wine for you?"

"A Shiraz would be nice."

I opened a bottle of wine while Mr. Stern got himself a wineglass. I poured wine in his glass and left the bottle open in case he wanted more. Cheddar had finished his supper and was licking his paws, so I washed Cheddar's food bowl and dried it while Mr. Stern sipped wine. Of the three occupants of the kitchen, Cheddar was the only one studiously not mentioning Ruby or Opal.

I got my grooming supplies and opened the french doors in the dining room. Cheddar came and stood on the threshold, half in and half out, peering into the garden as if he'd never seen it before.

I scooped him up, closed the door, and sat down in one of the deck chairs by the koi pond. Shorthairs don't need daily combing, but they enjoy it and it helps keep loose hair from shedding on the furniture. I took out my slicker brush and combed his throat with the short strokes cats love, careful not to let the bristles dig into his skin, then quickly moved over his entire body. Cheddar gave an annoyed swish of his tail, so I went back to his throat to soothe him.

Mr. Stern came out holding a plastic cup filled with koi food. Stone-faced, he leaned over the pond and sprinkled food on the water's surface as koi came swarming to the spot. He watched them gulp the floating food for a moment before he sat down in a deck chair.

He said, "Koi don't have stomachs so they can't eat much at one time. If they do, they'll die."

Cheddar and I watched a yellow butterfly sail over Mr. Stern's head, then flit to a mound of lobelia.

He said, "Filtration is even more important than food. Koi can live for weeks without eating, but they'll die in an hour in bad water."

Cheddar jumped from my lap to the brick floor, then into Mr. Stern's lap. Mr. Stern's hand rose in automatic response and stroked Cheddar's back. Cheddar reared on his back legs and put his front paws on Mr. Stern's shoulders, nosing his chin and purring loudly. Mr. Stern's lips threatened to smile.

Looking into Cheddar's eyes, he said, "My daughter died when Ruby was in high school. Ovarian cancer. She was only forty. Beryl was her name. After that, Ruby lived with my wife and me, but I couldn't control her. Drugs, bad crowd, all that. My wife died a year after Beryl. Broken heart, I think."

Cheddar stretched his neck and ran the tip of his tongue across Mr. Stern's chin. Mr. Stern smiled and bent to rub his nose against Cheddar's forehead. Speaking directly to Cheddar, he said, "Ruby started hanging out with the witch next door. The two of them got thick as thieves. Ruby moved out, didn't go to college, I didn't see much of her. I don't know how she came to be mixed up with that race car fellow, but she married him. At least she said she did, I never was sure if she was telling the truth."

Cheddar tipped his head and rubbed the top of it against the underside of Mr. Stern's chin. Mr. Stern's lips pinched into a straight line as if he regretted letting Cheddar know how painful his thoughts were. "She came home when the baby was just a few weeks old. I don't know if she left him or he left her. That's when she brought Cheddar."

I told myself to get up and walk away. I told myself I shouldn't be listening to a man's personal anguish, but my feet were rooted to the courtyard floor.

Still looking at Cheddar, he said, "She didn't stay long. One day she just took Opal and went away. I don't know where she's been. I called that Zack fellow but he claimed he didn't know where she was either."

I said, "What about Ruby's father?"

My voice seemed to startle him. "He was killed in Iraq."

His voice quivered, and he turned his head away. Apparently, Mr. Stern felt he had lost a son as well as a wife and daughter.

I gathered my grooming supplies and stood up. It was time for me to go. The situation in this house was laced with legal, emotional, and familial complications that were way over my head. Ruby and Mr. Stern needed a good lawyer and a good family therapist, not the unavailing sympathy of a pet sitter.

I said, "Is there anything else I can do for you before I leave?"

He shook his head, and I left quickly. We both pretended he didn't have tears in his eyes.

# 9

In the kitchen, Ruby stood holding Opal and turning side to side. New parents always seem to think babies want to be jiggled or rocked or swayed. I'll bet if they asked the babies, most of them would vote to stay still.

She said, "Opal's teething, I think. She was awake most of the night."

I went to the refrigerator and pushed the lever to release an ice cube into my hand, then folded the ice into a corner of a clean dish towel and smashed it with a cutting board.

I held out my arms and Ruby handed Opal to me as if she'd been waiting for me to work some kind of magic. With Opal cuddled close against my chest, I offered her the cold towel and her swollen gums seized on it like a baby bird grabbing a fat worm from its mother's beak.

I brushed the downy blond sprouts on Opal's head and breathed in the irresistible scent of clean baby skin. "When my little girl was teething, she liked to chew on cold things like this. A damp washcloth left in the freezer will work too."

Ruby grinned at the way Opal was gnawing on the towel. "How old is your little girl?"

I felt the familiar reluctance to answer, coupled with an unwillingness to deny my child's truth. "She was killed when she was three."

"Oh, God. How did you stand it?"

"For a long time, I didn't. I went crazy for a while. My husband was killed at the same time. It was almost four years ago. An old man hit the accelerator instead of the brake and crashed into them. It happened in a Publix parking lot, and for two years I couldn't buy groceries at that store."

Ruby's eyes glistened. "I don't think I could go on living if anything happened to Opal. I never knew how much you can *love* until I had her. It's not like any other kind of love, not like loving a man or loving your parents or your friends. It's like this little demanding person is your *breath,* and you'd die without it."

Every time I talked to Ruby, I liked her more.

As if she understood that her mother was talking about her, Opal gave me a shy, gummy smile. There's nothing in the world like a baby's smile to make you feel better about the human race. Babies don't smile to manipulate or ingratiate, they just smile because they come with a reservoir of smiles inside them and they pass them out with bounteous generosity. Opal's smile made my heart expand. She truly was an adorable baby, and I wanted to hold her in my arms forever.

I said, "She has beautiful eyes."

"She has Zack's eyes. That dark blue that's almost purple, and those long thick eyelashes."

She reached for Opal, and Opal's arms immediately turned toward the person she trusted most in all the world. I felt a momentary pain that I would never again see that look of absolute trust in my own child's eyes.

Ruby said, "Granddad thinks Zack is low-life, but he doesn't understand drag racing. Of course, Granddad thinks I'm low-life, too."

"Actions speak louder than words. Your granddad left Opal's crib set up in your old bedroom. That cancels out a lot of what he says."

She half smiled. "I guess it does. I can't remember Granddad ever telling me he loved me. I doubt he ever told my mother or grandmother he loved them, either, but I know he did. I think he just never learned how to show love, you know? That's why I got Cheddar for him."

"I thought Cheddar was your cat."

She shook her head. "I told Granddad he was, but I got Cheddar at the Cat Depot so he could love something he couldn't boss around."

I grinned. "From what I've seen, Cheddar has trained him very well."

"I lived with him and Granna after my mom died, and it was awful. If I was ten minutes late coming home, he acted like I'd been out whoring or shooting up heroin. If I didn't get all As on my report card, he carried on like I was destined to live in a Dumpster. After Granna died, it got worse. If it hadn't been for the woman next door, I would have gone crazy. Myra was the only person who believed in me, the only one who offered me a hand. Granddad never has forgiven her for it."

Carefully, I said, "I saw a woman looking out the window next door when I was here this morning. Mr. Stern and I were in the courtyard and she was watching us."

Ruby's face tightened. "That's Myra Kreigle. I'm sure you know who she is. I worked for Myra, and I'm a witness in her trial. I don't want her to know I'm here."

"But she's the woman who was good to you?"

"She was good to me *then*. People can be good and bad, you know? Nobody's all bad."

I remembered the venomous hatred on Myra's face as she looked down at me, and wasn't sure I could believe Myra had a good side.

I said, "There were two women, actually. A young one and an older one. Does Myra have a daughter?"

She shook her head. "I was the closest thing she's ever had to a daughter, and I didn't last."

Opal whimpered, and I handed over the towel with the cold, wet corner. But it had lost its appeal, so Ruby put her bent forefinger in Opal's mouth to gum.

Ruby said, "When I was a senior in high school, Myra started paying me to solicit rich men. Not solicit like a hooker, but circulate at her investment parties, talk to them, make them feel like they were big important hotshots, like I was really blown away by a man with so much money. I would put my hand on their arm, you know, lean in to show some cleavage, tell them how Myra was making a lot of money for other men, make it sound like I was more impressed with those other men because they were making so much more money. And then I'd ask them why they weren't letting Myra make them richer too, and offer to get them into her hottest investments. Most of them fell all over themselves getting in. It was funny, really, to see them scramble to impress me. Like they thought they were buying me when they gave Myra money."

"Did you know how she made her money?"

She looked away. "Not at first. I still don't know exactly how she did it, but over time she got careless about talking in front of me and I picked up little clues that her investment deal wasn't what she claimed."

She took a deep breath. "A lot of investors got money back, more than they'd put in. Every time a new person put money in, there was more money to pay out to the ones who wanted to collect their profits."

"And the more you hustled them, the more new people invested."

"Something like that."

Opal whimpered and moved from Ruby's finger to gnaw on her collarbone.

She said, "Until a few months ago, I'd never even heard the term *Ponzi scheme*. All I knew was that Myra paid me good money to go to her seminars and flirt with old rich men. I never slept with any of them, I never went out with any of them. Well, I did go out with some of them, but not anybody serious except Zack. I would have gone out with him even if he hadn't put money in Myra's investment trust."

Okay, now I was beginning to get the picture. Zack was one of the pigeons Ruby had enticed into Myra's trap.

"Did you ever tell Zack that Myra's investment was a scam?"

"Myra promised me he would get all his money back. She guaranteed it."

Feeling as if a boulder was balanced on my shoulders, I said, "Ruby, it isn't any of my business, but does the DA who's prosecuting Myra Kreigle know where you are?"

Sounding proud, she said, "I've been meeting with him for several weeks, telling him what I heard, what I saw. He came to see me before he filed charges against Myra, and then he found me a place to stay so she couldn't get at me. We worked out a plea bargain deal. I'll tell what I know about Myra's business, especially where she put the money, and I won't be charged with helping her."

The look in her eyes was as trusting and naïve as Opal's.

I already knew the answer, but I had to ask the question. "Does Zack know you've been cooperating with the DA?"

"Zack thinks I was part of Myra's deal. He thinks I lied to him, that I only married him for his money." With a firming of her jaw, she said, "I guess he'll sing a different tune after he hears me testify."

I had a bad taste in my mouth. Ruby was half street-wise sucker-bait and half babe in the woods. And her woods were filled with cruel traps. Myra had used her to entice men to invest in her phony scheme, the DA had used her to build a case against Myra, and she believed with all her twenty-year-old heart that Zack would know she truly loved him when he heard her turn state's witness against Myra. I could almost see the vision she had of Zack swooping her up in his arms and striding out of the courtroom like Richard Gere in *An Officer and a*

*Gentleman* while the audience cheered and Myra was hauled off to jail.

I said, "Do you know somebody named Vern? Or a man named Kantor Tucker?"

For a moment, I could see a family resemblance to Mr. Stern in the cool wariness on her face. "Why did you ask me that?"

"This morning when I left here, three men in a limo followed me to my next stop and grabbed me. They bound my ankles and wrists, put tape on my mouth and a hood over my head, and took me to a man named Kantor Tucker. The driver of the limo was a man named Vern. He told Tucker he'd seen me leaving here. I believe he thought I was you."

Ruby had gone pale. She closed her eyes and lowered her forehead on the top of Opal's head as if seeking strength.

She said, "Vern is Tuck's muscle. Sometimes he works for Myra."

"I'm older than you, but we look a lot alike. Same height, same size, same coloring. When Myra saw me in the courtyard with your grandfather, she must have thought you had returned. She probably called Vern and told him to grab you and take you to Tucker."

For an instant, Ruby tilted slightly to the side like a blighted tree. Fear or guilt or shame made her speech slurred. "How did you get away from him?"

"When Tucker got a look at me, he said, 'That's not her!' and sent Vern away. Vern didn't hurt me, and he gave me cab fare when he let me out. But they must be watching for you."

The french doors opened and Mr. Stern came inside carrying Cheddar. He stopped when he saw Ruby and me in the kitchen. He must have been able to read our faces and know something had just passed between us, but we turned to him with false smiles, and the moment passed.

Mr. Stern seemed more relaxed, perhaps because Cheddar was sending him love purrs. Or perhaps because he had unloaded some of his pain in the courtyard. Whatever the reason, he let me leave without directing me out of the driveway.

At least he and Cheddar had benefited from my visit. But Opal's gums were still sore and swollen, and I'd given Ruby reason to be frightened.

As for me, I was also frightened. Not for myself, but for Ruby. Now I was sure that Vern had thought I was Ruby when he grabbed me. And I was afraid I knew the answer to the question of what would have happened to Ruby if he'd got her instead of me.

The only bright spot I could find in the dark cloud that seemed to be hovering over Ruby and Opal was that the people who had sent Vern to kidnap Ruby would surely know by now that I'd told her they'd got me instead. They would expect her to be on guard now, which should discourage them from trying anything again.

That's what I tried to make myself believe. Every now and then I succeeded.

# 10

On the way home, I shared the street with bikers in skin-hugging Lycra shorts and shiny skull-protecting helmets. On the sidewalks, Roller-blading parents maneuvered baby strollers between kids trying to ollie on skateboards. In front of me, a tourist couple in a too-clean red Jeep surveyed the world with self-conscious smiles. His shorts were crisp khaki, his knit shirt was white, and his pale legs wore telltale black socks with sneakers. Her shorts were iron-creased yellow linen, her shirt was floral, and she wore a new straw boater with a rhinestone band.

At the firehouse where Beach Road intersects with Midnight Pass, two firefighters were in the driveway polishing a fire truck's chrome, while another firefighter was on the lawn tossing a Frisbee to a Doberman. The fireman tossing the Frisbee was my brother, Michael. The Doberman was Reggie, a courageous dog whose humans had been brutally murdered the year before. Reggie and I had saved each other from similar fates, and when

Michael and his fellow firefighters learned that Reggie had been left homeless, they'd taken him in as the official firehouse dog. Reggie had settled into the firehouse routine as if he'd been training all his life to live with a bunch of big burly guys who played with him and fed him and occasionally jumped into long pants and boots and drove off in a screaming red truck.

When I pulled into the drive behind the fire truck, men and dog all turned their heads with identical expressions—a mixture of hopeful anticipation of pleasant diversion and annoyance at having their fun interrupted. When they saw it was me, they all smiled, and Reggie wagged his stump of a tail. Maybe some of the men did too, I couldn't tell.

I slid out of the Bronco and Reggie ran to kiss my knees while Michael strolled to meet me with his face creased in a big grin. Like Paco, Michael is the kind of man who causes otherwise intelligent women to go weak-kneed with basic lust. He's blond and blue-eyed and his solid muscle is so bulky that he automatically swivels sideways going through doors. He's a firefighter the way our father was, a guy other firemen know they can depend on no matter how bad the situation is. He's also the kindest, most gentle man in the universe, and my best friend.

He glanced at my swollen lips, blushed, and looked away, obviously jumping to Tom Hale's conclusion that I'd been kissing too hard.

I said, "I thought I'd drop off a new tug-toy for Reggie."

One of the guys polishing the truck said, "Good! Reggie goes through those things fast."

I went around to the back of the Bronco and pulled two of the toys from a box of pet toys I keep back there. Mostly the toys aren't purchased, but mundane things dogs or cats like to play with. Dogs especially like braided tug-toys that are dirt cheap and dead easy to make from strips of flannel. I buy red plaid flannel blankets from Walmart—pets seem to like bright colors best—and cut them into strips about five inches wide and a yard long. Then I tie three strips together at their ends and tightly braid them. When the braided end is knotted, it makes a perfect toy for a dog to carry around or for a game of tug-of-war with a human. Since it's flannel, the tug-toy doesn't fray and leave strings lying around, and when the dog destroys it, you can make another one in no time from the same blanket.

I tossed a fresh tug-toy to Reggie, who immediately trotted off like a conquering hero with it gripped in his jaws.

As if they'd had the same thought at the same time, the other two firemen zipped to the truck's cab and pulled out a metal box.

Michael said, "We have something cool to show you."

The three men surrounded me while Michael opened the box. "It's an oxygen mask for animals. Somebody donated one for every fire truck in Sarasota County. It'll fit over an animal snout as small as a kitten's or as big as a Great Dane's. Uses the same oxygen tanks that EMTs use for humans."

Reverently, as if it were something holy, I touched the mask with a fingertip. When a house is burning, pets may die of smoke inhalation because they crawl into small spaces in an attempt to escape the heat. The new oxygen masks would undoubtedly save pets' lives.

I said, "Wow."

The men nodded solemnly, and replaced the box in the truck. They carried it as if it were the ark of the covenant.

I said, "Somebody donated masks to every fire truck?"

With one voice, the men said the woman's name. They spoke it with the same reverence they'd shown the mask. For a moment we were all still with the knowledge that any fool can cause deaths, but only the very special cause life.

Reggie ran up to Michael with the tug-toy dangling from his mouth and whuffed, a clear announcement that he'd been patient with human conversation long enough, and that it was time to get on with the important things in life, like playing. I gave the top of his head a quick smooch, and did the same to Michael's cheek.

I said, "I'll see you tomorrow."

"I may fill in tomorrow for one of the other guys. His kids want to go to Disney World before school starts, and it's the only weekend his wife can get off. We're taking turns, so tomorrow may be my day."

That's part of a fireman's life, doing double shifts occasionally for a buddy. Sometimes it means more sleepless hours fighting fires and sometimes it's merely another twenty-four hours of boredom. For Michael, it means cooking three more meals at work instead of at home. For Paco and me, it means the firefighters get the good stuff and we have to fend for ourselves.

Michael is the cook in our family. Since he was four and

I was two and our mother went off on a bender while our dad was on duty at the firehouse, Michael has assumed that it was his duty to feed me. He's also the cook at the firehouse. No matter where Michael is, he's the cook. He cooks the way poets write, with passion and tender ruthlessness. Paco and I eat the way poetry lovers read, savoring every nuance down to our very souls.

I got home just as the setting sun stained the sky crimson. Paco was on the deck with Ella in his arms, both of them watching the sun hover below a low wisp of cloud cover. Paco is tall, slim in the places a man should be slim, and broad in the places a man should be broad, like a triangle. He's Greek-American, but with his dark hair and eyes and olive skin he can pass for Caribbean, Middle Eastern, or Hispanic. Since he works undercover for SIB—Sarasota County's Special Investigative Bureau— the ability to look like a lot of different races and nationalities comes in handy. But Paco isn't just a pretty face who can infiltrate criminal organizations in disguise, he's also smarter than about ninety-nine percent of the people in the world. Sometimes he's so smart he's scary. But most important of all is that he loves my brother, and by extension, me. Paco and I are family.

I hurried across the sand between the carport and the deck to join him and Ella. They both gave me a quick look, then turned their attention back to the sunset. Our sunsets are the most spectacular in the world, so most people on Siesta Key can be found outside every evening watching the sun slip beneath the sea. It's always the same, but always different, and we don't want to miss any of its variations.

Tonight the pulsing edges of the sun were tinted burgundy as if they had gotten bruised on the way down. In the sun's glow, an undulating rose-hued highway stretched across the silver water to our beach like a red carpet of invitation. For a long moment, the sun hung lazily above the water as if it had forgotten it was supposed to drop below the horizon. A V of seabirds flew across the sun's face and, startled and embarrassed, it slid into the sea.

We watched the radiant sky a few more minutes, and then the spell broke.

Paco said, "Red sky at night, sailor's delight."

I nodded as if he'd just said something sage and wise, even though Paco isn't a sailor and neither am I. We just like to pull up old bits of almanac wisdom like red sunsets foretelling dry weather.

Paco said, "I heard you made some new friends today, kidnappers and such."

I said, "That would be a guy named Vern."

"What are you doing for dinner?"

That was another new thing about my PG—post-Guidry—status. Before Guidry became a significant part of my life, Paco and I had always taken it for granted that we would share dinner on the nights Michael was at the firehouse and we were both home. When Michael was home, we took it for granted that he would cook for us and that the three of us would sit down together and eat what he cooked.

But now in my PG status, Paco didn't know if I had plans to be with Guidry so he was unaccustomedly tentative with me. And since I was torn between wanting to be with Guidry and feeling defensive about the want, I tried to sound as if I had never even considered the possibility of dinner with him. The truth was that he hadn't mentioned it, and neither had I. We were both so new to this couple thing that we hadn't settled into any routine yet. I hoped we never would. I hoped we would, and soon. I was a mess.

I said, "I don't have any plans. Do you?"

"How do you feel about Mexican?"

"*Me gusto* Mexican. Give me fifteen minutes to shower and change."

Leaving Paco and Ella on the deck, I loped off to wash away cat hair and dog spit.

Being the world's fastest shower-taker, I was dressed in a denim miniskirt and white scoop-neck knit top within my promised time. I'd even pulled my hair into a knot at the back of my head with some long hairs hanging out to look fetchingly artless, and slicked some lip gloss on my tender lips. Big gold hoop earrings and high-heeled mules gave me just the right balance between slutty and stylish, and got me an approvingly raised eyebrow from Paco.

We didn't talk about my kidnapping until we were at El Toro Bravo, our favorite mom-and-pop Mexican place on Stickney Point. We opted for an outside table, accepted cold mugs of beer, crispy fried tortilla chips, salsa and guacamole from the waitress, and ordered platters of our favorite things smothered in chili, cheese, and extra jalapeños.

While we waited, Paco said, "Okay, tell me."

I gave him the CliffsNotes version. "Three guys in a limo grabbed me in the parking lot at the Village Diner. Two guys in ski masks rode with me in the back, the driver didn't have a mask. They bound my wrists and ankles with duct tape and put a hood over my head. They took me east of I-Seventy-five to that wealthy area where everybody's house has its own private landing strip and hangar. A man called Tuck came to the car and the driver said, 'I got her,' meaning me. Tuck looked in at me and said, 'That's not her.' Vern was the driver's name. Dumb as a stump, and mean. Tuck told Vern to fix the problem, also meaning me. So Vern drove me to Friendly's on Sixty-four and put me out in the parking lot. He told me he would deny anything happened if I reported it, and that I'd be in big trouble."

Paco dipped a tortilla chip in the guacamole and studied it as if he might find insight in it. "Guidry made you report it, didn't he?"

"He said as an officer of the law he had to report it. Now there'll be stuff in the newspaper about me again."

He gave a dismissive wave of the tortilla. "I wouldn't worry about it. Some reports of criminal behavior are confidential. Especially if there's an ongoing investigation."

A weight lifted from my shoulders. "I went to the Ringling office and looked at mug shots. I didn't see any that looked like Vern, but I know who Vern thought I was."

The waitress came wearing padded mitts and carrying metal platters holding bubbling chili-drenched food. As she set the plates down, she said, "The plates are very hot. *Very* hot."

She always says that. Like idiots, Paco and I compulsively touched the plates anyway. We always do that. Then we jerked our hands away because, like the waitress had warned, those plates were plenty hot.

After we'd gone through the initial ritual of forking up bites so hot we had to fan our mouths and cool them with beer, Paco said, "Who did they think you were?"

I told him about Ruby, and how Ruby had worked for Myra Kreigle pulling rich men into her Ponzi scheme.

"She said Vern was Tucker's muscle, and that he sometimes works for Myra."

Paco blew on a forkful of enchilada. "Vern is Vernon Brogher. Vern's a relative of some sort to Tucker, cousin or something. Works as a bouncer in a strip joint on the north Trail, drives limos for movie stars who come for the Film Festival, generally moves around job to job. He's been in jail a few times for being drunk and disorderly, fighting in bars, that kind of thing. Word is that Vern sucks up to Tucker and Tucker throws him a bone now and then because he's a relative."

I had a mental image of Paco and Guidry standing over the desks of the deputies investigating my kidnapping and soaking up every bit of information.

I said, "What about the other men with Vern? The ones in the ski masks?"

"Last I heard, they hadn't got results back from IAFIS yet."

I said, "Ruby has a baby. Looks about four or five months old, a real cutie. Her name is Opal. Ruby is married to a race car driver named Zack."

Paco nodded. "Zack Carlyle."

What is it about men and race cars? I'd never heard of Zack Carlyle, but I had the feeling I could go stand in the middle of the street and say "Zack!" and every man for miles would know who he was.

I said, "I always thought a drag race was two hot rods on a downtown street illegally racing."

"Actually, it's very expensive gutted-up old cars driven by professional racers on a legal drag strip. Very short course, very fast cars. Zack Carlyle is a champion Pro Stock racer. His uncle is Webster Carlyle, who's sort of a drag race legend. Webster's retired, but I guess he was a big influence on Zack, bigger than his father anyway. The father owns an electrical supply company in Bradenton, and Zack works for him. From all accounts, the father isn't keen on his son spending so much money on a hobby like racing, but Zack makes most of it back in prize money, so I guess the dad can't complain too much. From all accounts, Zack's a solid, stand-up guy. He runs a camp for disadvantaged kids, and he's persuaded a lot of professional racers and other athletes to come out and work with them. They have a little racetrack, run kid-sized racers around it. The kids have fun and learn about timing, sportsmanship, things like that."

I took a sip of beer and parsed what Paco had just told me. Zack's father was a successful businessman, Zack was a successful athlete, and there probably was some tension between them. I wondered if Zack's father had approved of Ruby as a daughter-in-law.

I said, "Zack and Ruby are separated. Mr. Stern doesn't know if she left Zack or Zack left her, but she came home when Opal was just a few weeks old and then left again without telling Mr. Stern where she was going. According to Ruby, the DA had put her someplace where Myra and Tucker couldn't get at her. She and the DA worked out a plea bargain deal and she's going to testify against Myra."

Paco raised an eyebrow. "If Ruby knows where Myra stashed the money she stole, she could do a lot of damage to Myra. Which means Myra has several hundred million reasons to try to keep Ruby from testifying."

A beat went by. I wondered if Paco knew more than he was telling. I wondered if Ruby was as innocent as she'd seemed.

I said, "Zack thinks Ruby was in cahoots with Myra, but Ruby expects him to change his mind after she tells the truth in Myra's trial."

Paco looked skeptical. "Zack Carlyle's organization for kids put about a quarter of a million in Myra's real estate investment trust. He and the other athletes had big plans for expanding the kids' program. Myra sent out false monthly reports showing their original investment had doubled. The reports were all lies, of course, and their money is down the drain. If Ruby knew the reports were false and kept quiet, he has good reason to be mad at her."

I thought of Myra Kreigle's hate-filled face looking down at me, and decided not to mention it to Paco. "No matter how the trial goes, it won't change anything for all the people who've lost jobs and homes because of Myra."

"Dixie, don't get involved in this mess. White-collar criminals are just as violent as any other kind. They'll kill you just as quickly if you get in their way."

"I'm just taking care of Mr. Stern's cat. Now that Vern knows I'm not Ruby, he won't bother me again. He probably won't bother Ruby, either. He knows she'll be watching for him now."

"People like Vern and Tucker and Myra Kreigle have been hurting people since humans stood upright. The only way to be safe from them is to stay away from them."

"I promise I'm not involved."

As I said it, I saw Opal's trusting face. Adults can use common sense to keep themselves safe, but who will keep babies like Opal safe?

# 11

While Paco and I ate dinner, the sky had darkened to the color of a newborn baby's eyes, with a lackadaisical gathering of stars punching weak holes in its vault. As we rounded the last curve on the drive to our house, we caught the glint of thin moonlight bouncing off Guidry's Blazer parked beside the carport. Paco chuckled softly and waggled his eyebrows at me. I poked him in the side, but it was hard to look angry with my lips turned up at the corners. Paco parked in his space and we both climbed out of the car.

He said, " 'Night."

I said, "Thanks for dinner."

Neither of us looked up at my balcony where we both knew Guidry waited. Paco walked briskly to his kitchen door and disappeared inside. I climbed the stairs to my apartment. I did not run, I walked normally. Well, I may have taken them a little faster than usual, but I definitely didn't run.

In the shadowy darkness of my covered porch, Guidry

was almost invisible. With his hands folded over his chest and his legs crossed at the ankle, he was asleep in the hammock strung in the corner. It was a rare opportunity to memorize his face without him knowing, so I stood quietly looking down at him. Except for his chest rising and falling, he looked like a corpse. A very healthy, bronzed corpse.

Around us, the night spoke with the soft chirps of tree frogs, the questioning whistles of ospreys, and tremulous wails of tiny screech owls. The sea seemed to hold its breath waiting for the evening tide.

As if he sensed my presence, Guidry opened his eyes, smiled, and reached for me. I stretched out beside him, the hammock rolled, and we ended up in a tangle of arms and legs on the porch floor, my laughter smothered under his lips. I gave a fleeting thought to the Mexican food on my breath, and then forgot it.

The moon smiled, the tide chuckled, the stars drew closer to watch, and at the end of time our hearts lay bare under an infinite sky, no longer separate from time and space but melded at the limit of love.

Later, behind Guidry's sleeping shoulders in my narrow bed, I allowed my mind to acknowledge that my happiness had tears in it. Allowed myself to remember the weeks after Todd was killed, how I had inhaled his scent, pressed his shirts against my face, pushed the fabric close to my nose and sobbed. For a long time I hadn't been able to sleep without him beside me. Death removes the smells, the sounds, the feel of the other that gives them life, so I hadn't wanted to eat or bathe for fear I would lose the scent of him and have no more memories of him in my pores.

And now another man was in my bed, and I was inhaling him the way I had once inhaled Todd, and it was good and right that he was there. Pain was still with me, but there was more sweetness than pain. New love had come as quietly as cats' paws, silent as smoke or trickling sand. It had drifted into my consciousness when I least expected it, shoving out memory of old loves, lost loves, hopeless loves, wrong loves, betrayed loves, true love, all fading into the darkness of doesn't matter. This new love stood alone, marvelous and electric, always believed in but never expected. The lightning it created lit up the universe from eternity to infinity, and lit up my heart from edge to open.

I moved closer to Guidry and pressed my cheek against his bare back. In the night's space, the touch of his skin made me feel safe. I drifted to sleep knowing that moment was the only thing that mattered, the only truth I needed to hold fast.

# 12

My daily schedule is set so firmly that I could do it in my sleep. A time or two I may have. I roll out of bed when my alarm rings at four A.M., splash water on my face, brush my teeth, and pull my hair into a ponytail. Still half asleep, I drag on shorts and a T, lace up fresh white Keds—I can't stand yesterday's sweaty shoes—and head out to walk the dogs on my schedule. Dogs can't wait the way cats can, so they get first dibs. Next I call on the cats. Maybe an occasional rabbit, ferret, or guinea pig. No snakes. I refer all snake-sitting jobs to other people. Not that I have anything against critters without feet, but it creeps me out to drop little mice into yawning snakes' mouths.

Leaving a drowsy man in my bed is definitely not part of my routine, and it felt weird to do it. Even though I'm thirty-three years old and have every right to have a man in my bed any time I choose to, I sort of hoped this was the day Michael would pull an extra shift at the firehouse. Otherwise, he might have come home before Guidry left and know he'd spent the night. Michael respects my right to live my own life, but he's a bit of a Victorian prude where I'm concerned.

The sky was a stretch of dull blue felt, with a few pale dawdling stars. On the horizon, night had lifted her dark skirt a few inches to let in a shimmer of pale pink day. Along the shoreline, surf babies were tumbling while mother sea slept unaware. The air smelled of ocean and first beginnings, and dew diamonds turned trees and flowers into fairy fantasies. On the porch railing, a slumbering snowy egret trembled at my presence and opened his topaz eyes to monitor my intentions.

Moving slowly so as not to alarm him, I went down the stairs to my Bronco, shooed a sleeping pelican and a young egret from the hood, and got myself back into a professional mode. Spending the night with a man is a surefire way to make a woman's career go to dead bottom on her list of priorities.

Starting at the south end of the Key and working my way north, I did my usual run with Billy Elliot and the other dogs. Then I reversed direction and called on cat clients, which on that day included three mixed-breed cats who'd been left alone while their humans went on a cruise, a pair of Siamese who'd only been left for a day while their humans were at the hospital welcoming a new baby, and several single cats whose humans were away for reasons none of the cats thought were good enough.

As I was leaving the house of one of the single cats, I saw two women getting out of a van next door. They were taking cleaning supplies from the van, and one woman seemed to be having a personal fight with a rebellious vacuum hose. I was at my Bronco before I recognized them as the cleaning women I'd seen the day before at Mr. Stern's house. The woman who'd been crying wasn't with them. Since they worked for Mr. Stern and I worked for Mr. Stern, and since I was pretty sure that Mr. Stern had been rude to her, I sort of felt a sisterly compulsion to go speak to them, maybe try to smooth things over so they wouldn't think badly of our mutual employer. I caught up with them before they got to the front door, and they both turned to me with the annoyed looks people give missionaries out ringing doorbells.

I said, "Hi, I'm Dixie Hemingway. I'm taking care of Mr. Stern's cat while his arm heals. You clean for him, don't you?"

They both studied me for a moment, still waiting for a punch line that would cost them something. Finally the older one said, "I remember you. You were going in when we were leaving."

The other one said, "Everywhere we go people have cats. We vacuum up more cat hair than anything else. Ruins the motors. This here vacuum is almost brand-new and it's already running hard from all the cat hair."

I said, "I know your friend got upset because of the baby at Mr. Stern's house. I hope she's okay."

The older woman scowled. "We don't know because Doreen didn't show up this morning. We always meet in the Target parking lot, but she never showed. I called and called, but she didn't answer her phone, so I don't know what to think."

The other woman said, "Doreen had a baby a couple of months ago, but it only lived a few hours, and she's been real emotional ever since. Then her boyfriend left her, and that about put her over the edge."

The older woman shook her head. "She's better off without him, if you ask me. He never was any help to her, didn't even help with her doctor bills."

I began half-stepping backwards, wishing I hadn't started this conversation. "Well, I just wanted to say 'Hi,' you know, since we all work in the same house."

They stopped talking and stared at me, once again looking suspicious. Neither of them said goodbye, but watched me get in the Bronco and back out. I waved goodbye, but they didn't wave back. I did a silent groan, imagining them quitting their job with Mr. Stern and telling him it was because I'd followed them and spied on them.

For about the millionth time in my life, I had followed an impulsive urge to be friendly to a stranger who had reacted as if I were a CIA operative trying to frame them for a crime. I try not to follow those impulsive urges, but the wisdom of sailing on by is always more obvious after the fact than before it.

The sun was fully up and the morning's moisture had dried on every leaf by the time I got to Mr. Stern's house. When I rang the doorbell, Ruby let me in. Her skin looked dry and chapped, and she had blue shadows under her eyes.

She said, "I just put Opal down for a nap, thank God. She was awake half the night. Cheddar's in the bedroom with her." With a sudden conspiratorial grin, she said, "Come see!"

All her fatigue seemed to fly away as she skittered down the hallway ahead of me. She was like a teenager leading a girlfriend to see her latest secret, and I was reminded again of how young she was. With exaggerated stealth, she turned the bedroom doorknob and pulled the door open just enough for me to look inside the room.

When I peeked in, I grinned, too. Opal was sound asleep in her net-sided crib. Under the crib, Cheddar slept in a shallow cardboard box. The box was a bit too small for his entire body, so one of his paws flopped over the edge in boneless bliss.

Ruby said, "Is it okay to leave him there until Opal wakes up?"

I knew exactly how she felt. When you've finally got a baby to go to sleep, you don't want to do anything that might wake her.

I said, "If Cheddar lived in the wild, he would eat whenever he found food, not at some special hour."

She said, "Granddad's in the courtyard feeding the koi."

I wasn't sure whether she was merely relaying information or hoping I'd keep Cheddar's delayed breakfast a secret from Mr. Stern.

She followed me into the kitchen and watched me shake dry food into Cheddar's clean feeding dish. It would be ready for him whenever he and Opal finished their naps.

I got eggs from the refrigerator and put them in a pan. "Mr. Stern likes me to coddle an egg for Cheddar and boil a couple for him."

"It's nice of you to do that."

I covered the eggs with water and set them on a burner. The impulsive urge to tell her that I knew Mr. Stern was wrong to doubt that she was truly married to Zack Carlyle drifted across my cortex and then stopped itself before it came out my mouth. I'd already followed one impulsive urge to speak about something that day, two would be pushing it.

But my brain must have exercised all the control it could handle, because the next thing out of my mouth was even worse. "Ruby, was Kantor Tucker a partner in Myra's Ponzi scheme?"

"I don't know if he was a partner or just knew what Myra was doing and kept quiet."

"Now that you know how far they'll go to try to stop you from testifying, what are you going to do?"

The look she gave me was puzzled. "You mean kidnapping me?"

I resisted saying, "D'uh!" and nodded.

"Believe me, I already know how far they can go. Tuck had a guy cross him once and he flew him out over the Gulf and shoved him out of the plane. *That's* how far they'll go."

She said it flat-voiced, not like somebody repeating a terrible crime.

I said, "Are you sure of that?"

"I didn't see him do it, if that's what you mean, but he laughed with Myra about the guy being shark food. I don't think he was joking. If he thought he could get away with it, he'd feed me to the sharks too."

A cold snail moved up my spine leaving a slimy trail of dread. Ruby apparently had knowledge of other crimes besides fraud, knowledge that made her even more dangerous to Myra and Tucker.

"So what are you going to do at Myra's trial?"

"What I told the DA I'd do. I'll tell what I know."

Her young face was set in lines I'd seen on my own face too many times. Fierce courage mixed with the kind of faith that only comes from utter naivete. Sometimes that mixture moves mountains. Sometimes it creates an abyss that you walk into unaware.

I said, "What about Zack? Does he realize what's going on?"

She shook her head. "Zack's a Boy Scout. He believes the world is black and white, good and bad. He thinks I'm as bad as Myra. He wouldn't believe me if I told him the whole story."

A thin cry came from Ruby's bedroom, and we both froze. But it didn't continue. Opal had waked for a moment and cried, and then gone back to sleep. Babies do that, and Ruby and I gave each other relieved looks. Ruby was relieved because she was Opal's mother and attached to her in that mystical maternal way of all sensitive mothers. I was relieved because I felt too much of a connection to Ruby and Opal. Not just because Ruby and I looked alike, but because I *knew* her. Knew what it was to yearn for a lost mother, knew what it was to be too young or too dumb to intuitively recognize criminal behavior in someone I trusted. Knew what it was to fall head over heels in love with a good man and have his baby and be as close to it as to my own pulse beat.

The water on the eggs came to a boil, and I turned off the heat, set the timer for three minutes, and used a spoon to fish out Cheddar's egg.

I broke the coddled egg over the dry food in Cheddar's bowl and turned to face Ruby.

"Do you think Myra and Tuck will try anything else to stop you from testifying?"

"They might, but until the trial begins, I'm not leaving this house, not even to go in the courtyard. And if the doorbell rings, I'm not answering it unless I know who it is."

"A wise person once told me that white-collar criminals are as dangerous as any other criminals."

She met my eyes with a fearless directness. "Myra and Tuck would have me killed if they thought they could get away with it. But they can't. Besides, I've already given the DA enough information to convict Myra of every charge they've made against her."

Something about that line of reasoning seemed wrong, but while I searched for a response, the timer sounded and I hurried to lift Mr. Stern's eggs from the hot water.

Mr. Stern chose that moment to come in from the courtyard. With a disapproving look at Cheddar's food bowl, he said, "Where's Cheddar?"

Ruby said, "He's in my bedroom under Opal's crib. They're both sleeping."

He made a fitzing sound with his lips, not exactly a raspberry but close. I had the feeling his disapproval came more from jealousy than from concern about Cheddar's delayed breakfast.

As if he felt a need to reestablish his authority, he frowned at me. "Are you boiling eggs?"

"I just took them out."

"I'd like toast as well. Make it two. Buttered."

Ruby stared at Mr. Stern, and seemed to press her lips together to keep from speaking.

My own tongue probably got shorter because I had to bite it to keep from telling him that in the first place I wasn't his maid, and in the second place he was acting like a total butt. I scooped his eggs onto a plate and made his toast while he took a seat at the bar and watched me like a big brooding bird.

When I left him, my mind was stuck on the fact that Cheddar sleeping under Opal's crib was making Mr. Stern act like a jilted lover. For a man who claimed not to have any time to waste on a cat, his jealousy was a little bit funny. At least it would have been if he hadn't acted so snotty to Ruby. Of all the emotions human beings fall victim to, jealousy and possessiveness may be the most unattractive.

At the time, it didn't occur to me that it was Ruby, not Cheddar, who Mr. Stern believed had been stolen from him. Or that he resented that loss with a rancid hatred.

# 13

The tension at Mr. Stern's house hadn't changed the fact that I was empty as a koi without a stomach. Heading for the Village Diner for breakfast, I paid close attention to all the other cars on the street, especially the occasional limo. I didn't see anything suspicious. Even so, I sat a moment in the parking lot after I'd parked the Bronco just in case somebody was there planning to kidnap me.

I didn't intend to linger over breakfast. I wanted to get home and take a long nap and get wholly back into my own body. Having Guidry in my life was great, but I'd worked hard at arriving at a place where I was fairly content with who I was, and I didn't want anything about myself to change. It was another one of those boring versus comforting things.

Inside the diner, I waved at Tanisha on my way to the ladies' room. Tanisha's broad face dimpled when she saw me, and I knew she'd have my breakfast ready by the time I sat down in my regular booth. I liked that. I'm a lot more satisfied with life when it stays the same, day after day. Lots of people would find that boring, but I find it comforting.

Sure enough, after I'd washed up and got myself as presentable as possible in the ladies' room, Judy had a mug of coffee ready for me. Like Tanisha, Judy is a good friend I only know through the diner. Judy is tall and angular, with light brown hair that frizzes in the steam from Tanisha's kitchen, eyes that change from hazel to Weimaraner amber, and a sprinkle of copper freckles across her nose. She's cynical and snarky and loses her heart to men who hurt her. She was kind to me when I lost most of my mind after Todd and Christy were killed, and she was the first person to predict that Guidry and I would wind up together.

As I slid into the booth, she said, "Missed you yesterday."

I said, "Yeah, I got kidnapped."

She grinned and scooted off to pour somebody else some coffee. I am the kind of person whose life is so weird that people think I'm joking when I tell the truth about it. If I'd told her that I'd just come from a house where a woman was up to her eyebrows in a Ponzi scheme trial, she probably would have laughed her head off.

Judy had just returned with my breakfast when Guidry ambled down the aisle and slid into the seat opposite me. Judy stood aside and watched us, and I knew she could see us exchange the looks of people seeing each other for the first time after they've spent the night together. A look that combines a residue of pleasure, a hint of embarrassment at having let down all their defenses, and a frisson of excitement at the hope they'll repeat it.

Guidry said, "I'll have what she's having."

Deadpan, Judy said, "With bacon?"

He grinned. "Oh yeah, I forgot she never orders bacon."

Judy said, "She just steals it off other people's plates."

I shrugged because it was true. I love bacon beyond reason. If I get a choice of a last meal before I leave this planet, I'm going to order a BLT with extra-crispy bacon, no icky white bumps anywhere in it, no curled ends, no droopy middles. I rarely order bacon because it's bad for my health and for my waistline, but everybody knows that fat doesn't settle on you if you eat it from somebody else's plate.

Judy left a mug of coffee for Guidry and hurried away to turn in his order. He and I gave each other the self-conscious grins of two people who'd slept coiled together like strands of a rope.

I sipped coffee and looked at him through the steam.

"I talked to Ruby this morning while I was at Mr. Stern's house—he's her grandfather, has an orange cat named Cheddar, lives next door to Myra Kreigle—and she said she's not sure if Kantor Tucker was a full partner in Myra Kreigle's fake REIT or if he just kept quiet about it."

Guidry's gray eyes studied me for a moment, and I knew he was having an internal conversation with himself about the way complete strangers told me highly personal and private things. Since his job was to get information from people, it made him nuts that people blabbed everything they knew to me. Sometimes when I didn't even ask them.

He said, "Tucker and Myra Kreigle have been connected for several years, maybe lovers, maybe partners in crime, maybe just good friends. If she leaves the country before her trial, he'll lose the two million dollars he put up for her bond."

"He has a private plane at his house. Maybe he'll fly her out of the country."

He grinned. "Not likely. He'd be met and arrested wherever he landed, and his plane would be confiscated. But she may have transferred two million to him from one of her hidden offshore accounts, so he won't really lose anything if she bolts. But if Ruby's testimony places Tucker in Myra Kreigle's deal, it could be his undoing."

I had an uneasy feeling that Guidry was placating me, that he really had something else on his mind that he wanted to talk about, but couldn't get up the nerve to say it.

Judy came with Guidry's breakfast, topped off both our coffees, and zipped away without speaking. I took one of Guidry's rigid slices of bacon. For a few minutes we were quiet. I nibbled my bacon while Guidry ate.

He said, "I had a friend in New Orleans who was a drag racer like Zack Carlyle. At least he was until he got a detached retina from the jolt of decelerating too fast."

"You're kidding, right?"

"Some of those cars go faster than a space shuttle launch. They have to use parachutes to stop. You go from three hundred thirty miles an hour to a dead stop in less than twenty seconds, and it'll cause a drag up to five Gs. My friend did that and it caused his retina to detach. His wife said she would be the next thing to detach if he raced again, so he quit."

I said, "Ruby said Zack has dark blue eyes that are almost purple. The baby has his eyes."

I could tell Guidry didn't give a gnat's patootie about Zack's eyes. His mind had drifted someplace else. He finished eating, took a last gulp of coffee, put money on the table for Judy, and got to his feet.

He did that shoulder-tapping thing again. "See you later."

Judy came with her coffeepot and we watched him leave. I seemed to be watching his back a lot these days. Which wasn't bad, with those shoulders and the easy way he moved. But it still made me uneasy to see him leaving, as if every time was the last time I'd ever see him.

It occurred to me that whenever Guidry mentioned New Orleans, his voice took on a longing quality. Like a man speaking the name of a woman he'd once deeply loved and lost. Or a woman he'd once loved and wanted back.

I was still thinking about that when I headed for the Bronco, so engrossed in all the awful possibilities of the idea that I almost walked into Ethan Crane. Ethan is a tall, drop-dead gorgeous attorney with jet-black hair and dark eyes from Seminole ancestors. When I saw him in front of me, we did that self-conscious side-stepping dance that men and women do who were never lovers but once had the hots for each other. To tell the truth, we sort of still did, but we had both decided that somebody else was really more appropriate for us. Another attorney for

Ethan, another cop for me. I had met Ethan's new girl-friend, and he knew Guidry. We approved of the other's choice, but my hormones still stood up and applauded when they smelled Ethan, and from the way his eyes lit up when he saw me, I suspected certain parts of his anatomy were also standing up.

We stood in the glaring sun and bantered a little bit, nothing important, just the usual awkward small talk people do to try to cover up the fact that they really want to ask each other more important questions. Like *Do you miss me?* Like *Are you happy with somebody else?* Like *Do you ever regret your choice?* My answer would have been that I was happy with Guidry and I had no regrets, but I sort of hoped that Ethan sometimes regretted his.

When we said goodbye, I felt that odd exhilaration that comes with knowing you've spent time with a man who thinks you're desirable. Even if you don't want him, it's exciting to know he wants you.

At home, Paco's truck was gone, but Michael's car was in his slot. Instead of going straight upstairs, I walked across the sandy yard to the wooden deck and opened his kitchen door. When he and Paco had moved into our grandparents' house, they remodeled the kitchen to bring it into the twenty-first century. A butcher block eating island with a salad sink at one end stands where our grandmother's round pedestal table once took center stage, and Michael has added enough Sub-Zero built-in refrigerators to hold all the fruits and vegetables at any farmer's market, plus two or three steers.

When I walked in, he was leaning over a refrigerator

drawer forcing a stalk of celery to fit into a space already filled with other vegetables.

He looked over his shoulder at me. "Hey."

Ella Fitzgerald was on her assigned stool. She and the guys have an agreement—if she stays on the stool and doesn't beg for food, she can sit there and adore them. I smooched the top of her head.

I said, "I want you to hear this from me."

Michael straightened and looked down at me with eyes that had suddenly gone slitty. "Hear what?"

"Well, here's the thing, I'm here and I'm obviously okay. So it's not important, but it happened, and I know sooner or later you'll hear about it, so I just want to be the one to tell you."

His eyes got slittier. Ella sat up straighter and looked alarmed.

I said, "The thing is, yesterday morning a guy named Vern mistook me for a woman named Ruby and drove me out past Seventy-five to that stretch of big estates where everybody has a landing strip and a hangar. He took me to a man named Kantor Tucker, but as soon as Tucker saw me he knew I was the wrong woman. Vern drove me to Friendly's and gave me fifty dollars for a cab. I called Guidry and he came and got me. That's all there was to it."

"So Vern just asked you nicely to get in his car, and you did, and he drove you to a place where a stranger could get a look at you. Is that how it was?"

"Pretty much. I'm taking care of Ruby's grandfather's cat, and I guess Vern saw me leaving there and jumped to the conclusion that I was Ruby. She's a witness in Myra

Kreigle's trial. You know, the woman who ran the real estate Ponzi scheme. Ruby worked for her."

"What else?"

"That's it, truly. Except for the part about the two guys in Vern's limo who grabbed me and put a hood over my head. Vern drove while they taped my wrists and ankles, and put tape over my mouth. But they didn't hurt me, Michael. They overpowered me, but they didn't rough me up or anything."

Michael's lips weren't relaxed anymore, and a muscle worked in his jaw. "So what did Guidry do?"

"He made me report it. I went to the office on Ringling and looked at mug shots. I didn't see anybody that looked like Vern, but the guys investigating already know who he is. He works for Tucker, sort of a hanger-on. They don't know who the other men were, but the deputies have the tape that was put on my mouth. They're running latents from it through IAFIS to see if they get a match."

Michael walked around the butcher block island a few times, like a man on the deck of a ship that he can't get off of. Ella watched him with big round eyes.

"So what's going to happen now? Is Guidry taking care of this?"

Michael's tone said that if Guidry wasn't doing his job, Michael would.

I said, "Guidry's in homicide, so he's not part of the official investigation, but he's involved. So is Paco."

"Paco knows about this?"

"Yeah, we had dinner together last night and I told him."

He looked a little hurt, so I hurried to tell him about Ruby being married to Zack Carlyle.

He brightened. "Zack Carlyle? No kidding."

He said it as if Zack Carlyle went around wearing a red cape and leaping over tall buildings.

At least I'd got his mind off Vern kidnapping me.

Upstairs, Guidry had neatly made up my bed before he left. I found it sort of touching that he'd gone to the trouble. After a shower, a nap, and some time spent updating my client records, I cleaned my apartment. I got rid of every speck of dust, every smear on a mirror, every dull haze on anything chrome. I polished and disinfected and vacuumed until I was high on bleach and ammonia fumes. My brother handles stress by cooking. I handle it by cleaning the heck out of everything. My brain tells me that bad things can happen to people with clean apartments, but my Scandinavian genes tell me that cleanliness and order are as good as a horseshoe over the door. They protect you even if you don't believe in them.

As I put away the vacuum, I heard a peculiar tapping noise coming from my kitchen window. A female cardinal was obsessively flying at the glass and hitting it with her chest and beak while the male flew in anxious circles behind her. Cardinals do that sometimes during springtime nesting when one sees its reflection and thinks it's another bird invading its territory. But this was September, not a time of building nests, so the female's attack on her own image seemed out of the natural order of things. I wondered if the bird was afraid a rival female was on the periphery of her territory ready to move in. Whatever her reason, the cardinal attacked her own image with the intention of keeping a tight hold on what was her own. A noble purpose, perhaps, but she could kill herself.

I stood for a while and shooed her away. Every time I left the window, she came back to do her kamikaze dives at the glass. I taped paper to the glass, but it didn't stop her. I found a magazine picture of a glaring owl and taped it to the glass, but she wasn't fooled. While I dressed for afternoon rounds, the sound of her beak hitting the glass was like the relentless sound of a ticking clock. I had mental images of her beak splitting down its length and making it impossible for her to eat.

When it was time to leave my apartment to make afternoon rounds, I was acutely conscious that a bird was slowly committing suicide at my kitchen window. On the sandy shore, a few gulls, terns, and sandpipers braved the glaring sun to pick up microscopic nutrients from the lapping sea, their subdued cries like doleful omens. Driving slowly, so as not to disturb the songbirds and parakeets taking siestas in the trees lining the drive, I was all the way to Midnight Pass Road before I got myself under control. Nature has been getting along without my direction since the beginning of time. The cardinal would either give up her attacks on her reflection or she wouldn't. In either case, I had done all I could do to save her.

Nevertheless, I had a skitty feeling that the cardinal carried some sort of message for me, a woman-to-woman bit of wisdom. But I wasn't flinging myself against a hard surface that would hurt me, and I didn't believe that some other female was trying to steal my mate. At least I didn't know of one.

# 14

At Tom Hale's condo, Billy Elliot met me at the door with a big grin. Tom was in the kitchen with his laptop open on the table.

He yelled, "I want to show you something."

As if he wanted to make sure I stayed focused on my reason for being there, Billy Elliot walked close beside me to the kitchen. Tom pointed at a photograph on the computer screen.

"Is this the guy who kidnapped you?"

In a newspaper photo, Vern and Kantor Tucker stood in front of an airplane, Vern a little bit behind Tucker. They were both smiling, Tucker more broadly than Vern. The caption read, "Kantor Tucker at his aero-compound." An accompanying article identified the plane as a new Boeing 707, the latest addition to "Tuck" Tucker's private fleet of planes. There was no mention of Vern.

I said, "That's Vern."

Tom said, "Here's another picture." He clicked some

keys and the screen filled with a mug shot of Vern's bruised, sullen face.

He said, "This is from Indiana, a year or so ago. His name is Vernon Brogher. He was arrested after he slammed a guy's head into a wall in a bar. The guy had asked him to stop taking cellphone photos of the guy's girlfriend, and Vern nearly took the guy's head off. Literally."

"Is he a pilot?"

Tom snorted. "I don't imagine Vern is smart enough to fly a paper airplane, much less a jet."

"Ruby said he's Tucker's muscle."

"Does that mean he's Tucker's bodyguard or the man who beats up people for him?"

"With Vern's history, it probably means both. How'd you find those pictures?"

"If you spend enough time on the Internet, you can find anything, especially things of public record."

Billy Elliot leaned against my knees to remind me that time was passing. Tom watched me snap Billy's leash on his collar.

I said, "Do you know anything about drag racing? The professional kind?"

"You taking it up?"

"Ruby is married to Zack Carlyle. He's a drag racer. You know, one of those guys who race around on a track."

His face took on the look of a kid hearing about a really cool video game.

He said, "Drag racers don't go around on a track, Dixie. A drag race is a straight shot and it only lasts a little over four seconds. Two cars at a time race over and over, until one car has beat out all the others in its class."

I said, "Hunh." No matter what Tom told me, I kept imagining a line of cars tearing around an oval track. I couldn't wrap my mind around the idea of a straight race that lasted only four seconds.

Billy Elliot whuffed to remind me that I was there to run with him, not to chat with Tom, so I led Billy out to the elevator in the hall.

When we came back upstairs, I unsnapped Billy Elliot's leash and waved goodbye to Tom.

He said, "How'd you like to go to a drag race? You and Guidry, me and Jennie."

It seemed like every being in the world was either in a new relationship, like the humans I knew, or fighting to keep a relationship, like the self-destructive cardinal flying into my kitchen window. I guess some relationships bring serenity and some bring desperation.

Jennie was Tom's new girlfriend, and she had passed my test of worthiness by running on the beach with Billy Elliot. But I wasn't sure if Guidry and I were at a double-dating stage yet. Joining another twosome makes a different kind of statement than doing things alone as a couple. I wasn't sure what the statement was, but I didn't think we were ready to make it yet.

I said, "I'm sure Guidry would like to go to a drag race, but I don't think drag racing is my thing."

I didn't say it, but what I thought was that Zack Carlyle might be a name that men got excited about, but as far as I was concerned, he was a man who had failed the test of loyalty to his wife and baby.

Tom said, "It might not be a good idea anyway. Those guys who grabbed you may have something to do with drag racing, and men who kidnap women off the street aren't usually the kind of men who'd appreciate her following them. Especially if she's following them with a cop."

"They wouldn't know Guidry is a cop. He doesn't look like a cop."

Tom's eyes got a pitying look. "Dixie, even Billy Elliot could look at Guidry and know he's a cop. Cops look like cops. They can't help it. They have cop eyes and cop mouths, they move like cops. Believe me, you go to a racetrack anywhere in the world with Guidry, and half the people there will take one look at him and remember pressing engagements elsewhere."

For the rest of the afternoon, I thought about what Tom had said. When I looked at Guidry, I didn't see a cop, but it was true that cops get a look in the eyes that people in other professions don't have. A watchful look. Not like rangers scanning the horizon for forest fires or like store detectives on the lookout for shoplifters. More like a three-hundred-sixty-degree awareness of everything going on around them even when they aren't looking directly at it. I had to admit that Guidry had that look. If we went to a racetrack where Vern and his buddies were, they might recognize the look. If they did, it might scare them enough to leave the county, which would be fine with me.

As I pulled into Mr. Stern's driveway, I instinctively looked upward at the Kreigle house next door. No face was in a window looking down at me. I hoped the sad young woman had gone someplace where she would be happier.

Inside the Stern house, a new tension rode on the air. Ruby was silent and grim, Mr. Stern was on the phone in the kitchen. Even Opal seemed to have pulled inside herself.

As I shook dry food into Cheddar's bowl, Mr. Stern spoke to Ruby as if they were mid-conversation. "You're a big girl, Ruby, and you know how to use the phone. You're not doomed to starve just because I've ordered food for myself."

She said, "I know that, Granddad. It just seems peculiar for a person to order dinner delivered without asking the other person in the house if she'd like something too."

"I guess I got so used to not seeing you or hearing from you that it just slipped my mind that you were here."

Ruby's eyes flooded and she left the kitchen with Opal hugged tightly to her chest.

I didn't speak. Just left Mr. Stern in the kitchen to sulk alone. I cleaned Cheddar's litter box while he ate, then went back to the kitchen and washed and dried his bowls. I put fresh water in his water bowl and left the kitchen with my lips squeezed shut. Mr. Stern had a waiting empty wineglass on the bar, but he didn't ask me to open a bottle of wine for him, and I didn't offer.

Outside Ruby's bedroom door, I tapped lightly and called her name. Her "Come in" was muffled, as if she'd had her face buried in a pillow. When I went in, she was sitting on the edge of the bed. Opal was in her crib watching the play of late sunshine on the wall.

I said, "This is my last stop for the day, and I'm going

home to have dinner with my brother and his partner. My brother is the best cook in the world. Would you and Opal like to join us?"

She looked so grateful that I had to avert my eyes so she wouldn't see the pity in them. "Do I need to change clothes?"

"Heck no, we're barefoot diners."

"I'll just put a clean Onesie on Opal."

I waited, thinking how young mothers may go out of the house looking like yesterday's warmed-up oatmeal, but they want their babies to always look cute.

Before we left, Ruby ducked into the kitchen. "I'm going out with Dixie for dinner, Granddad. Can I have a house key?"

Taken by surprise, he muttered something I couldn't hear, and when Ruby joined me at the front door she held a door key in her hand.

On the way to my place, neither of us spoke of the tension in Mr. Stern's house, or of the fact that he was treating her shabbily. Neither did we speak of Myra Kreigle, of the trial, or of Vern. Instead, we talked about people on the street, the clothes they wore, the clothes movie stars and celebrities wore, the shops in Sarasota where women could buy those kind of clothes. Trivial woman talk to avoid deep woman talk.

At home, Michael and Paco accepted a guest lugging a baby with graceful equanimity. Paco hurried to set an extra plate on the redwood table on the deck, and Michael made the kind of admiring noises at Opal that warm the cockles of a mother's heart. I left them on the deck to get acquainted while I zipped upstairs to shower and get into clean shorts and a T. When I came downstairs, Paco had Opal in his arms and Ruby was helping Michael carry food from the kitchen.

For a moment I felt as if I were looking at a slice of life preserved in the amber of time, with the baby being Christy, Ruby being me, and Todd a numinous presence somewhere in the shadows. The moment passed and we were just people getting acquainted—a woman who was a younger version of myself, a baby who was like my own child who had died, Michael and Paco who had always been there for me, and the wrenching memory of my beloved husband.

Ella did not share my bittersweet feelings. Ever since she had given Paco a scare by bounding into the trees while we ate, he had decreed that she would wear a light harness with a cotton leash looped around the leg of a lounge chair. She had come to tolerate that indignity, but she watched Michael and Paco fawning over the baby with the gimlet-eyed imperiousness of the Red Queen.

Dinner began with a cup of lentil soup with a squeeze of lemon to give it a lift. Michael whirred up a tiny bit in the blender for Opal and got a flirtatious flutter of eyelashes and a drooly smile. No matter how young or old, every female falls for Michael.

After the soup, Michael brought out poached Alaskan salmon with dill sauce, baby red potatoes, and a salad of cucumber, orange, and Florida avocado. Hot french bread and a crisp white wine made just the right finishing touch.

Over dinner, Michael and Paco and I kept the conversation moving, tossing topics around like beach volleyball players with the easy familiarity of people who know one another extremely well and speak a kind of code that doesn't have to be explained. We talked of inconsequential things—the weather, a funny scene Paco had witnessed on the street, Michael's buddy at the firehouse who had taken his family to Disney World.

"We're taking turns filling in for him," he told Ruby. "My day will be tomorrow."

Ruby didn't care what Michael's schedule was—why would she?—but Paco and I nodded like business executives noting a significant change in plan. I didn't know if Ruby was aware of how diligently we worked to avoid speaking of Myra Kreigle or her trial.

Dessert was big chunks of sweet watermelon, the real kind with black shiny seeds and honest flavor. Ruby let Opal gum a tiny bite, but she mostly drooled red juice on her Onesie, and the new experience of watermelon made her cry. Opal had enjoyed as much of new acquaintances as she could stand.

I said, "I think it's time to drive you home."

Ruby smiled. "If you don't mind. It's past Opal's bedtime."

While Ruby gathered up the diaper bag and said her thank-yous and goodnights to Michael, Paco slipped inside the house to put on shoes. He followed us to the carport and climbed into his dented truck. "I'll follow you."

His voice didn't leave any room for discussion, which made me realize that in addition to adding shoes to his attire, he'd probably also added a few loaded guns. I looked toward the deck, where Michael was busily gathering up leftovers and chatting with Ella. He and Paco had come to a decision they hadn't discussed with me, and the decision was that Paco would stick to us like glue and make sure nothing happened to Ruby on the way home.

If Ruby found it unusual to have an armed deputy riding on our bumper, she didn't mention it. At Mr. Stern's house, I pulled into the driveway and left the motor running while Ruby gathered her baby paraphernalia. Opal was fussy, but Ruby leaned across to hug me before she slid out of the car. "Thanks, Dixie. I appreciate that dinner more than you can ever know."

She slammed the car door closed and scurried toward the front door, with Paco close behind her. He waited until she had unlocked the door and disappeared inside, then glided past me to his truck. On the drive home, he stuck close to me, and it occurred to me that he was guarding me as carefully as he'd guarded Ruby. It was a disquieting thought.

Back home, I waved a thank-you to Paco and headed up my stairs while he ambled across the yard to his back door. I was inside my apartment before I realized he'd ambled with deliberate slowness to give me time to get inside. Another disquieting thought. I didn't believe I was in danger, but apparently Paco thought it was a possibility.

A wave of exhaustion hit me as I got ready for bed, and I crawled between the sheets with the kind of mind fog that comes from too much thinking. Even so, I was still thinking. I wondered how long it would take Ruby to recover from the trauma of the last several years of her life. From what Mr. Stern had said, Ruby's life had taken a sharp turn when she was in her early teens. Within two or three years, her mother had died a lingering death, her father had been killed in a war, her grandmother had died of heartache, and Ruby had been left with a grandfather who was incapable of showing affection. In her pain, she had turned to Myra Kreigle as a mother substitute. In her naivete, she had let Myra use her to defraud other people. With the same need for love that we all have, she had believed she had found it with a race car driver named Zack Carlyle. Zack had turned against her when he lost all the money he'd invested with Myra Kreigle, and Myra was willing to destroy Ruby to save herself.

I wondered what any individual's limit is. How much pain and loss can any of us absorb before we collapse? I knew what my own limit was, and I knew every person has his or her own limit. Ruby had taken more hard knocks than most women could take, even women a lot older, but I knew a moment would inevitably come when she couldn't take any more.

If I ran the world, every adult would get several time-outs from life. The time-outs would come about every twenty years, and each one would last five years. Five years to recover from school or marriage or parenthood or career or war or grief. Five years to cry or sleep or pray or stare at the wall. A roof and a bed would be provided, along with an unlimited supply of wholesome food, musical instruments, and books. No drugs, alcohol, or tobacco would be allowed. No therapists or religious proselytizers. At the end of five years, recovered lifers would swear an oath to give more thought to the four Fs—family, friends, food, and fun—than to career goals, achievements, possessions, status, or bank statements.

When sleep managed to shut up my thinking mind,

my dream mind took over and sent me to a gift shop so posh and out of my league that I was embarrassed to pollute it with my presence. I didn't have any choice, though. Under dream rules, I had to buy a gift for Guidry and I had to buy it at that particular shop.

I said, "I want to buy a gift for someone important to me."

As soon as the words left my lips, I felt my face flush. The female salesclerk, who looked like Myra Kreigle but was somebody else, gave me a pitying look.

"Would that be a male or female? Adult or child?"

My face got even hotter. I should have thought this out before I came in.

"Male," I said. "Adult."

"Aha," she said, as if I'd gone beyond her expectations. "Now, is this adult male a coworker, a family friend, a relative, or a lover?" The sneer in her voice implied that it was highly unlikely I had a lover.

Now my face was so hot I knew I had turned an unlovely magenta. I had to get this conversation under control. *My* control, and the way to do that seemed to call for pretending not to be Guidry's lover.

"More like a friend who might conceivably become a lover. Someday. Maybe."

She gave me a coolly appraising look and I knew she was wondering how anybody as incoherent as I had ever managed to meet a man like that. Meanwhile, my face had got flaming hot because I'd used the word *conceivably*, as in *conceive*, as in get pregnant not by asexual means.

She said, "Does he have any hobbies that you know of?"

Clearly, she doubted I knew a man well enough to

know if he had hobbies. I felt insulted, but the truth was that if Guidry had any hobbies, I didn't know what they were.

I said the only thing that came to mind. "He's from New Orleans."

She nodded, the way people encourage awkward children, but she disappeared without suggesting an appropriate gift. I was left feeling I'd missed the only opportunity I'd ever have to give something valuable to Guidry.

# 15

I woke the next morning feeling as if a weight had rolled off me while I slept. I still felt that Ruby and I were kindred spirits, but Ruby's load was her own to carry, not mine. The law of cause and effect creates strict boundaries in every person's life, and Ruby was experiencing the effects of her own decisions and actions. I could sympathize with her and be of help to her, but I knew I could not and should not interfere in her life. Furthermore, I was a pet sitter. My job was to empty Cheddar's litter box, not to imagine myself mother to Opal or big sister to Ruby. Mr. Stern was Ruby's grandfather, and even though he had behaved like a prize boob the day before, I believed he was a better man than he acted, and that he cared for Ruby and Opal. They would all be okay without my hand-wringing concern.

Going downstairs to the Bronco, I whisper-sang off-key, "You're entirely way too fine, entirely way too fine, get me all worked up like that, entirely way too fine, da-da-da-di-da, um-hunh." Lucinda Williams will never fear competition from me. The air had a salty, sandy, fishy Gulf smell, the fragrance of life. The sky was fleecy, with a thin disc of retreating moon hanging over a pewter sea. On the pale shoreline, as if to echo my whispered song, a sighing surf foamed scalloped designs onto the sand. A great blue heron asleep on the hood of my Bronco extracted his plumed head from under his wing when he heard my song, gave me a red-rimmed glare of indignation, stretched his wings to their full six-foot span, and flapped away with the muted sound of an avalanche. All in all, a normal, run-of-the-mill, predawn morning on the Key.

The rest of the morning was typical. The horizon pinked at the right time, glowed apricot on cue, and ever so subtly transmuted itself into a smooth pale blue canvas for the day's artistry. Gulls gathered into balletic groups to swoop and wheel against the sky's blue scrim, terns and egrets got busy picking up tasty morsels on the ground, songbirds trilled and chirped just because they felt like it. Billy Elliot and I did our regular run, and then I went house to house feeding cats, grooming cats, playing with cats. I was so efficient, so cheerful, so *good*, I could have been the star of a documentary about pet sitting.

Even Mr. Stern's sulkiness didn't faze me. When I got to his house, Ruby opened the door. She looked happier, and I hoped it was because she'd escaped stress for a little while the night before.

She rolled her eyes toward the kitchen in a sort of conspiratorial way to let me know that Mr. Stern could hear us. "Cheddar's with Opal again. He slept under the crib last night and he's been in the bedroom all morning. Opal looks for him when he's not there. It's funny how they've bonded."

I didn't imagine Mr. Stern thought it was funny. I had an image of him sitting alone in the dark courtyard, watching the play of light on the waterfall without Cheddar in his lap.

I bustled into the kitchen as if I didn't notice Mr. Stern's dour expression. He sat at his spot at the bar, waiting for me to arrive and boil his eggs, make his toast, pour him a cup of coffee from a pot heating on its pad on the counter. Mr. Stern was perfectly capable of boiling his own eggs, making his own toast, and pouring his own coffee. Jealousy of Cheddar's attachment to Opal had caused him to go infantile and demanding, traits he would have sneered at in anybody else.

Ruby drifted into the kitchen, poured herself a cup of coffee, and leaned against the counter to watch me cater to her grandfather's grouchy mood. I had the dance down pat: eggs in a pan, a pirouette to the sink for water on the eggs, another to set the pan on the stove. Two slices of bread in the toaster, set the darkness indicator, do an arabesque to the cupboard for the cat food, a plié to sprinkle dry food in the cat's bowl and set it on the floor. I felt so graceful and birdlike, it's a wonder I didn't break into canary song.

With Ruby and Mr. Stern as audience, I added Cheddar's coddled egg to his food, got out a plate for Mr. Stern, fished his soft-cooked eggs from the pan, and buttered his toast. But as I set Mr. Stern's breakfast on the bar, an uneasy awareness of something not right made me turn my head toward the bedroom wing. At the same moment, Ruby's head rose like a dog sniffing the air.

In the next instant we both whirled and ran.

Behind us, Mr. Stern shouted, "What is it? What's happening?"

I could smell it now, an acrid odor of smoke along with an oddly sweet scent.

I yelled, "Fire! Call nine-one-one!"

Down the hall, tongues of flame licked from under Ruby's closed bedroom door, and I could feel waves of heat emanating from it. Even with my mind in chaotic panic, I knew the intensity of that heat made no sense. It was too strong, too forceful, too driven. Heat of that magnitude could only be generated by a blaze that had been raging for a long time.

Ruby screamed and pushed past me to open the bedroom door. But before her clawing hand reached the knob, the door blew toward us as if it had been hit by a bomb. In its place was an impenetrable wall of raging fire.

Howling with panic, Ruby clambered over the door toward the roaring flames. I would have done the same if my baby had been on the other side of that wall of fire, but I caught her around the waist and pulled her back.

She twisted against me and beat at my hands. "Opal is in there!"

"We can't go through those flames! We'll have to go through the outside door!"

If she heard me, the words didn't register. Determined to go through fire to get to her baby, she clawed and kicked at me while I tried to drag her away from the doorway.

As if it had malevolent intelligence, the fire stood like a pillar from hell, its mighty force melting the paint on the door frame in cascading ripples that added a rubbery smell to the stench of smoldering wood.

Mr. Stern ran toward us, ineffectually yanking at his shoulder brace to try to free his injured arm.

I yelled, "Did you call nine-one-one?"

"Fire trucks are on their way!"

With one arm still immobile in its brace, he charged toward the flames with the same determination Ruby had.

I yelled, "You can't go in there, Mr. Stern!"

He stopped, but his rigid back said he was trying to figure out how best to dash through the flames and rescue his great-grandbaby. His carriage said he was a military man, he'd encountered fires before, he could handle this.

Fiery fingers reached through the doorway to stroke the wallpaper in the hall, and still he stood poised to run forward. Wild with terror, Ruby struggled against me like a feral creature. I could barely keep my hold on her. I couldn't fight them both. If Mr. Stern plunged into that furnace, I would not be able to stop him.

"Mr. Stern, please!"

With a shudder of broken acceptance, he turned toward me, reaching with his good arm to help me restrain Ruby. He meant to help, but the truth was that holding Ruby was definitely a two-handed job. Besides, I needed as much space as I could get, and he was in the way.

In my deputy voice, I shouted, "Stand aside, please!"

He looked shocked, then hurt, then nodded sad understanding. I had succeeded in reminding him that he was too old, too weak, and too useless to save either his great-grandbaby or his granddaughter. With a last sorrowful look at the inferno that had been Ruby's bedroom, he ran down the hall toward the kitchen.

"Mr. Stern, we have to get out of here!"

He yelled, "Not without Cheddar!"

I didn't have any breath left to argue with him. He had either forgotten that Cheddar had been in the bedroom with Opal, or he had slipped into denial.

My throat burned from the smoke, and my arms felt as if they were being pulled from their sockets. With my last shred of strength, I spun Ruby around so fast her feet left the floor. Kicking the air, she screamed and fought while I slogged her weight toward the front door. But I was no bigger or stronger than she, and I wasn't sure how much longer I could keep her from twisting away from me. If she did, she would die trying to save her baby.

The siren grew louder. Grimly holding on to Ruby, I floundered down the hall. At the front door, I shouted to Mr. Stern again, but got no answer. With one last burst of effort, I managed to hold Ruby with one arm and grab the doorknob and wrench it open with the other. Blessed fresh air hit my face, along with the sight of a fire truck pulling to the curb with uniformed firefighters spilling from it.

Michael was at the forefront, and as he ran up the driveway he looked so much like our father that I felt an out-of-time sense of history repeating itself. But our father had died saving a child's life, and I was sure the child in this house was already dead. No living being could survive the cauldron of fire that Ruby's bedroom had become.

Seeing me struggle with Ruby, he took her from me as if she were a rag doll and stood her on her feet. "Stay out of the house!"

Ruby's hair was wild, her face smudged with soot and smoke, her eyes all pupil, black and insane. "My baby's in there!"

Putting his face close to hers, Michael shouted, "Then don't get in the way while we put out the fire!"

She recoiled as if she'd been slapped, but her eyes focused and she didn't try to run back inside.

I said, "The fire's in a bedroom with an outside sliding door. There's a baby in the bedroom. Also a cat. And an elderly man in the kitchen. He's looking for the cat. He doesn't want to leave without him."

Other firefighters surged forward, and Michael barked information to them. "Outside slider to the bedroom where the fire is. Baby and cat in the bedroom, elderly man in the kitchen, irrational."

Within seconds, a fireman had gone in and brought Mr. Stern out the door, with orders to all of us to get as far away as possible. We huddled in a clump at the end of the driveway, staring wordlessly at the house. Ruby shook so violently that I put both arms around her and held her tightly, like swaddling an infant. Mr. Stern was pale as white marble, his eyes dry and staring as if he'd suffered a shock that left him unable to blink.

More sirens approached, more fire trucks jerked to a stop in front of the house, more firefighters appeared in their helmets and boots and uniforms. Two ambulances with EMTs came, along with a department car driven by a deputy fire chief. Across the street, neighbors had come outside to watch, clotted together as if to protect one another.

A woman ran across the street and put an arm around Ruby.

The woman said, "You shouldn't be this close, come across the street."

She and I half-carried Ruby while Mr. Stern followed like an obedient child. Other neighbors had spread quilts and pillows on the grass for people to sit on. My rational self was grateful for their kindness. My cynical self resented the way they seemed to prepare for an outdoor concert. My cynical self had misunderstood their intent. Instead of watching as if it were an entertaining event, the neighbors observed a solemn hush as if they were in church.

Ruby stared mutely for a while and then with an anguished howl toppled to the ground facedown. Wordlessly, women gathered beside her and stroked her back, their eyes meeting in silent pity above her devastated form. None of us could imagine a grief so shattering as Ruby felt. None of us could offer any solace or hope or comfort. All we could do was surround her with compassion. Mr. Stern sat alone, sending out waves of resistance that kept the neighbors away. I didn't approach him either. Every person grieves in his own way, and I respected Mr. Stern's right to suffer in solitude. He knew what had happened. He knew that there was no hope for either Opal or Cheddar.

I don't know how long we sat there. Time seemed to both speed up and slow to a crawl. I took it all in as if I were watching from a disincarnate distance.

After what seemed eons, Michael stepped from the front door cradling a small blanket-wrapped form in his arms.

# 16

A woman in the group said, "What's that fireman carrying? Is that a baby?"

Ruby scrambled to her feet. "Opal!"

Michael hurried to one of the ambulances where an EMT opened the back door.

With me close behind her, Ruby ran across the street and clutched Michael's sleeve. "My baby?"

He shook his head. "It's the cat."

He turned a corner of the blanket back to reveal Cheddar's limp form. He was not burned, but his eyes were closed and his mouth open, and I couldn't see any sign of breath.

Michael said, "I found him when I felt under the bed. At first I thought it was a stuffed toy."

Ruby turned to me with hope lighting her eyes. I knew what she was thinking: if Cheddar had escaped the flames, Opal might have too. But a cat can crawl under a bed when a room is afire. A four-month-old baby cannot.

Michael handed Cheddar to the EMT and ran back to

the house. The EMT climbed into the ambulance where a second EMT already had the pet oxygen mask ready to put over Cheddar's snout. When it was in place, Cheddar lay on the EMT's lap with a hose attached to an oxygen tank snaking over his limp body.

Across the street, Mr. Stern had managed to push himself up from the ground—not an easy feat with one arm in a sling. He moved toward us in jerky steps like a marionette whose strings needed adjusting. When he reached Ruby, he put his good arm around her shoulders. At his touch, Ruby sagged against his thin chest while he awkwardly patted her back.

One of the neighbor women ran to help Ruby back to her spot across the street.

Mr. Stern watched them go, then turned his attention to Cheddar. Only a fine tremor in his shoulders betrayed his despair.

I said, "Mr. Stern, the EMTs have a special oxygen mask for animals. They're using it on Cheddar."

"What about Opal?"

I had never heard him say the baby's name before.

"We don't know yet."

"So much *tzuris*," he muttered. "Such *tzuris*!"

I didn't know Yiddish, but the sound reflected the suffering and trouble around us.

Across the street, Ruby had folded to her knees and buried her face in her hands while neighbor women tried to comfort her. Watching them, I thought of the way Myra Kreigle had once mothered Ruby. I wondered if Myra was watching Ruby now from her second-story window.

After what seemed like an eon, the EMTs gave each

other tentative smiles. I hadn't seen a change in Cheddar, but the EMTs must have seen a twitch of his tail or a blink of his eye. Mr. Stern made a thin noise in his throat that told me he'd seen their smiles too. But that was all we had, that hint of possible success.

In a few minutes, we both saw the tip of Cheddar's tail lift, saw him paw at the oxygen mask, saw his eyes open. Mr. Stern's face crumpled into unashamed tears of joy.

A few more minutes, and they removed the oxygen mask and gently lifted Cheddar to his feet. He stood, stretched his tongue in a wide-mouthed yawn, then curled into a ball on the EMT's lap.

The second EMT stood up and spoke to Mr. Stern. "Sir, I think your cat's going to make it. He's breathing on his own, and he's able to stand up. We're going to take him to an animal clinic. You can ride with us, if you'd like."

Humbly, Mr. Stern said, "Thank you, young man." I'd never heard him be humble before.

I said, "I'll follow you in my car."

"No, you stay here with Ruby."

I didn't argue. Technically, my job was to help Mr. Stern take care of Cheddar, but I knew I would not be needed at the animal hospital. Ruby, on the other hand, needed all the help she could get.

I helped Mr. Stern into the ambulance and waited until it had driven away before I crossed the street to sit with Ruby.

Nobody spoke. We waited silently, staring fixedly at the house. One woman had her arm around Ruby's shoulders and I held Ruby's hand, but I doubted Ruby was aware of us.

A growling sound of an approaching muscle car intruded into the silence, the kind of sound you usually notice in the middle of the night and wonder who would be driving that fast at that hour. The sound made Ruby raise her head, and when the car sped to a stop in front of her, she got to her feet. The car was a sleek, black, low-slung foreign convertible that I didn't recognize. Two men were in it, one of them about as skinny and thin-skinned and blond as a Caucasian can get, with eyebrows and lashes so white they were almost invisible. He was young, midtwenties, and looked like the kind of kid that hadn't dated much in high school because he'd been more interested in physics or math.

The other guy was the exact opposite, as broad and black and tall as an African-American man can get. About the same age as the white guy, his head was shaved, his muscles bulged in all directions, and he had a face that would frighten criminals on death row. He and the white guy looked like mismatched peas in a shiny foreign pod.

Ruby made a soft bleating sound and stretched her hand forward, while the white guy looked at her with so much pain and anguish that it hurt to watch.

# 17

With neighbors looking on in rapt silence, the narrow white guy got out of the car and looked across its hood at Ruby, his face a cage holding in roiling emotions. The black guy heaved an impatient sigh, threw open his door, lumbered to Ruby, and enveloped her in his arms. He looked even bigger standing up. Having a brother as big as Michael has made me accustomed to wide shoulders and chests, but this guy was twice as big as Michael.

A spasm of envy crossed the white guy's face, but he seemed more envious of the other guy's ability to show feelings than jealous that Ruby was holding on to him as if he were a savior.

I stood up and waited, like a guard ready to leap into some possible fray.

The white guy walked around the car and stood beside me. "I came as soon as I heard."

Up close, he looked like a young Tom Petty, with a kind

of tensile strength under tender vulnerability. His eyes were so dark blue they were almost violet.

Ruby turned a wrecked face to him. "They haven't found Opal yet."

The white guy winced, and the black guy spun Ruby into the white guy's arms. He did it the way someone would move a dish from the soapy water to the rinse water, as if it were the right time. And Ruby and the white guy held one another as if they accepted the black guy's wisdom without question. Ruby began to keen, her mouth muffled against the man's chest, while he rocked her back and forth the same way she had rocked Opal.

The black guy turned to me and gave me a dimpled smile that was the sweetest expression I've ever seen on anybody over the age of two.

He said, "How do, ma'am. I'm Cupcake Trillin."

Now I understood why he kept his features arranged in a mean scowl. With a smile that sweet, he'd probably been given the name Cupcake when he was a baby, and grew up having to protect himself because of it.

"Pleased to meet you, Cupcake. I'm Dixie Hemingway. I'm here to help take care of Ruby's grandfather's cat."

My hand disappeared in his, and for a second I could feel the thrum of raw power zinging into my palm. Cupcake was the kind of man you wanted on your side, not playing on the enemy's team.

As if he wanted to make sure everybody understood what he meant, Cupcake raised his voice. "That man with Ruby *where he belongs* is her husband, Zack."

Letting a beat go by for everybody to absorb the full

import of both his words and the emphasis he gave to some of them, he said, "What's the story here?"

He was asking me, not Ruby. Ruby was too lost in her husband's arms to hear anything Cupcake said.

"The fire started in Ruby's bedroom where the baby was taking a nap. It came up suddenly and hugely. Ruby tried to go through a wall of flames, but I stopped her. I had to fight her to keep her from going in."

His eyes were steady on me, intelligent eyes that seemed to understand the entire situation in its entirety. He seemed about to ask me another question, but stopped when he saw Michael come out the front door and head toward us. I knew from the way Michael walked that he did not have good news.

If Michael wondered who Zack and Cupcake were, he didn't show it. He simply stopped in front of Ruby and waited a second to give her a chance to prepare herself. His eyes were very sad.

Speaking directly to Ruby, he said, "We didn't find the baby. I'm sorry."

Ruby swayed toward him, eating his words as if they had tangible form.

He said, "The fire was mostly contained to one spot in front of the bedroom door."

She said, "I don't understand."

Zack said, "He means somebody set the fire and took the baby."

Her voice rose to a hysterical pitch. "Is that what you're saying? Somebody took Opal?"

"We can't make that assessment until the investigators

rule out the possibility that she climbed out of her crib and found a hiding place we didn't uncover."

As if each word took superhuman effort, Ruby said, "She's only four months old. She isn't crawling yet."

Michael already knew that. He had held Opal on his lap the night before and fed her lentil soup. He knew exactly what the situation was. But he was not in charge of the investigation and he could only speak of what he knew as a firefighter on the scene.

He said, "We're calling for searchers to look for her."

Zack said, "It was arson." He was making a statement, not asking a question.

As soon as he said it, I knew it was true. Now I understood what the strange sweet odor had been. Somebody had put some sort of flammable concentrate in front of the bedroom door and set fire to it. While it raged, Opal had been taken from her crib, carried out the side door, and the door closed, trapping Cheddar inside the room.

Michael said, "I can't make a call about arson. That's for the fire marshall."

Conflicting emotions moved across Ruby's face like a string of disparate clouds. I knew what she was feeling, because I felt it myself. Michael was offering the possibility that Opal was alive.

Heavy with fatigue and sadness, Michael looked down at her. "As I said, we'll continue to search the house and grounds for the baby. But if nobody else was in the house . . . and if she couldn't get out of her crib by herself . . ."

As if she had suddenly remembered something terribly important, Ruby whipped her head to stare at Myra Kreigle's house. Understanding dawned in her eyes, and in an instant her soft young face hardened into a concrete mask of enraged hatred.

Jerking from Zack's arms, she raced across the street to Myra's closed door. As she ran, she unleashed a hoarse shriek that trailed her like a bloody shroud. I recognized that howl. It was the sound of anguished rage I had made when I learned that Christy had been killed, the betrayed sound every bereaved mother has made since time began, the cry that echoes forever unto the outer reaches of infinity.

I ran after her. When I was halfway up Myra's front walk, Ruby began banging and kicking the front door. "Open the door! Open the door or I'll knock it down!"

The door swished open, and I stopped where I was. Myra was so intent on Ruby that she didn't seem to register that I was there. Perhaps she was so sure of herself that she didn't care.

I had seen newspaper photos of Myra, and I'd seen her face at the upstairs window, but this was the first time I'd had a chance to see her up close. She was an imposing figure. At least a head taller than Ruby, she was whippet thin, with smoothly coiffed raven hair and the stark white complexion that some dramatic brunettes have.

Ruby shouted, "What have you done with Opal? Where is she?"

Myra's crimson lips stretched in a saccharine smile, and I had a momentary flash of being eight years old and feeling terror in my heart as I watched Cruella de Vil's malicious red lips curve on a movie screen.

"Why, Ruby, dear! Whatever is the matter? Have you gotten careless and misplaced your baby?"

Ruby shrieked and charged at her, but Myra stepped back and Kantor Tucker slipped into her space. With both arms stiffened, he grabbed Ruby's wrists.

Kicking at him, Ruby shouted, "Where is Opal?"

He twisted her wrists and leaned to bring his face close to hers. In an automatic reflex, my toes flexed against the pavement to push myself forward to help her. But the oily sound of Tucker's voice stopped me.

"I always thought you were a smart girl, Ruby. But a smart girl doesn't tell lies about people who've been good to her. A smart girl knows people who've been good to her will be good to her baby, too. Unless she's not smart. Unless she repeats those lies. Then her baby might end up with the sharks. You understand me, Ruby?"

For a long moment, we were all frozen in place. Then I moved to stand at Ruby's side. I didn't know what I could do for her, but she was too vulnerable standing alone. Tucker didn't show any more awareness of my presence than Myra had. I had the feeling I truly didn't exist for them. Myra and Tucker had their own little universe, and their rule of it was absolute.

Staring intently into Tucker's eyes, Ruby had gone almost as pale as Myra.

Through lips gone white with fear and futile rage, she whispered, "I understand."

Tucker released her wrists and cupped her hands in both his own. "There's our good girl! And we take care of our own, Ruby. You know that. We take very good care of our own."

Ruby whimpered a helpless cry as Myra came back to stand beside Kantor. She looked down at Ruby with an expression that seemed genuinely sad.

She said, "I was the only one who was good to you, Ruby. The only one."

Weeping softly, Ruby choked, "Yes. Yes, you were."

"You have broken my heart."

"I'm sorry. I'm sorry."

"We won't speak of it again. But you must trust me. You see? That's what life is all about, two people trusting each other to do the right thing."

"I understand."

With a triumphant glance at me, Myra stepped away from the door and Kantor pulled it closed. Ruby buried her face in her hands and sobbed, but there was a shred of relief in her tears, like a beggar grateful for a crust not tainted by mold.

My mouth tasted of ashes. I wasn't sure what had just happened, but I knew it was something terrible. Perhaps more terrible than arson or kidnapping.

Once, when I was a deputy, I had been present when a man had to be cut from an overturned tanker transporting gasoline. The man's foot was crushed under tons of metal, the tanker was smoldering and threatening to explode at any minute. The only way to save the man had been to amputate his foot. The tanker blew up seconds after the man had been removed to safety, and his face had worn the same mixture of unbearable loss and resigned acceptance that I saw on Ruby.

Zack and Cupcake crossed the street, both looking confused and wary. They had seen what happened, but they hadn't been able to hear what was said.

Zack said, "Ruby, what's going on? Do you think that Kreigle woman has something to do with Opal being taken?"

Ruby raised her head and stood with her hands clasped together like someone in prayer. The despair in her eyes was like a bleeding wound. A few hours before, she had been a pretty young woman. Now she looked old and haggard.

She said, "Myra didn't have anything to do with it. I just went a little crazy for a minute. I was wrong."

I was amazed at how easily and convincingly she lied. I was also amazed that she was protecting Myra. From the look that Zack and Cupcake exchanged, I got the feeling they knew she lied and weren't at all surprised by how well she did it.

# 18

While Zack and Cupcake and I stared at Ruby, each of us processing this latest piece of an increasingly strange puzzle, two cars screeched to a halt at the curb. One was a black sedan driven by a gray-haired man I'd never seen before. The other was a green-and-white from the Sarasota County Sheriff's Department. Mr. Stern's house was no longer strictly a firefighter's problem. The fire marshall would investigate the arson, and the sheriff's department would investigate the crime of child abduction. The fact that arson had been a cover for kidnapping would require the two departments to join forces. Like trying to get the FBI and the CIA to work together, that would either be a positive thing that would bring a quicker solution to the crimes, or a complication that would throw a wrench into the smooth workings of both units.

Sergeant Woodrow Owens slammed out of the sheriff's car, moving faster than I'd ever seen him move. A tall, lanky African-American officer, Owens usually moves like swamp water and talks like his tongue is wallowing a mouthful of buttered grits. He also has one of the quickest minds in the universe. I know because he was my superior when I was a deputy.

Two other sheriff's cars arrived in quick succession, and Owens stopped to speak a few terse words to them. The white-haired man from the other car came to stand in front of Zack and Ruby like a flagpole. His eyes cut disapproving slashes into Zack.

He said, "Son, haven't you gone through enough because of this woman?"

Stiffly, Zack said, "Dad, the baby's been kidnapped."

The older man's voice dripped ice. "Ruby, I'm sorry about your baby. But that's how life works. You lie down with dogs, you get up with fleas."

Zack's pale face flamed. "She's not just Ruby's baby. She's mine too."

His father's lip lifted in a sneer. "I wouldn't be too sure of that."

Ruby whirled toward him. "No wonder Zack doesn't know how to be a father to Opal! You've done everything you could to keep us from being a family, and you succeeded! But don't you dare imply that Opal isn't Zack's baby!"

Stung, Zack said, "How could I be a father to Opal when you took her and left? What was I supposed to do when I didn't even know where you were?"

Zack's father looked pleased, but Cupcake's brow creased like a worried hound's.

Cupcake said, "Look, folks, let's stay focused. There's a

missing baby. All that other stuff can be straightened out later."

Zack looked chagrined. "Cupcake's right. We have to find Opal and bring her home."

His father said, "Stay out of it, son. Let the cops handle it. That's their job. And for all you know, Ruby may have set it up herself. It wouldn't be the first time she's pulled a dishonest trick."

I expected Ruby to explode, but she merely gave her father-in-law an anguished look.

The knob of Adam's apple quivered in Zack's skinny neck, as if his voice had to climb over it to be heard. "Dad, I think it would be best if you left now. I understand how you feel, but I have to make some decisions and I need to make them without your help. Please."

The older man looked shocked, and I had the feeling he rarely heard Zack speak so forcefully. He contemplated his son as if he were a defective piece of merchandise. "We all know the kind of decisions you make without my help."

Zack stood straighter. "Dad, I'm asking you to leave. Please."

With an exasperated huff, Mr. Carlyle spun toward his car, turning back halfway there to say, "Just don't let yourself be pussy-whipped, boy."

Zack's face burned, and Cupcake's frown deepened. Ruby seemed too preoccupied with inner pain to notice the latest volley of scorn from her father-in-law.

Deputies began stringing crime scene tape around the yard, and Sergeant Owens headed toward Mr. Stern's front door. He saw me and stopped.

"Hell, Dixie, what are you doing here?"

"I'm taking care of a cat for Mr. Stern. He's the owner of the house. Has a torn bicep muscle."

His eyes raked my sooty clothes. "Were you in the fire?"

"A little bit, but I'm okay."

With a nod toward Ruby, I said, "This is Mr. Stern's granddaughter, Ruby Carlyle. She's the mother of the kidnapped baby. And this is the baby's father, Zack Carlyle."

A light glinted in his eyes. "Zack Carlyle." He rolled the name over his tongue like a connoisseur of fine wine tasting something rare and wonderful. I decided it was official. Every man in the world knew about Zack Carlyle.

He said, "Who was present when the fire started?"

I said, "I was here. Mr. Stern was here, and Ruby was here. Mr. Stern's cat suffered smoke inhalation, and the EMTs saved him. Mr. Stern has gone with the EMTs to take the cat to an animal hospital."

Zack said, "My friend and I heard about the fire on the news and came straight here."

Owens said, "The baby's disappearance was on the news?"

"No, just the fire. The house is next door to Myra Kreigle. That makes the fire newsworthy, I guess."

Owens didn't ask who Myra Kreigle was. Everybody in Sarasota knew what Myra had done.

To Ruby, he said, "Ma'am, do you know anybody who might have kidnapped your baby?"

She raised her head and spoke clearly. "I think it may

have been a cleaning woman who was here yesterday. She cried when she saw Opal, and the other women with her said she'd lost a baby a few months ago. She's the only person I can think of who would steal Opal."

I was stunned. Both at the logic of what she'd said, and at the ease with which she'd said it. But I had to admire the brilliance of the lie. The cleaning woman was a perfect suspect. Mothers who've recently lost their own babies can become so irrational in their grief that they take somebody else's baby. For a second, I even considered the possibility that the cleaning woman had actually stolen Opal. But only for a second. As soon as I remembered Tuck's chilling words to Ruby, I discounted the possibility of anybody other than one of his goons sneaking into the bedroom and snatching Opal from her crib. This wasn't about stealing a baby, it was about people with more power and money than the entire state making sure that Ruby didn't testify in Myra's trial.

Ruby looked at me with pleading eyes. I thought of Paco saying that white-collar criminals would kill as quickly as any other criminal. I thought of Tucker's plane, and of Ruby saying Tucker had flown a man over the Gulf and shoved his body out to be eaten by sharks. I thought of Tucker's slimy innuendo when he'd spoken to Ruby, the veiled threat that Opal might meet the same fate unless Ruby cooperated.

I said, "I talked to those cleaning women this morning. They were working at a house next door to one of my clients, but they said Doreen hadn't shown up for work today. That's her name, Doreen. She's obese. If you put out a bulletin to watch for a woman like that with a baby, add obesity to the description. About my height, but easily over two hundred pounds. Depression does that, you know. Puts on pounds. The other women said Doreen's boyfriend had left her after her baby died."

Ruby shot me a look of pure gratitude.

Owens grimaced. "He must be a stellar guy. Do either of you know the woman's last name?"

Ruby said, "You'll have to ask Granddad."

"Okay, I need to go inside the house for a minute and speak to the deputies in there. Mr. and Mrs. Carlyle, I'll need to get more information from you."

He looked a question at Cupcake, who shrugged his massive shoulders. "I'm just here as Zack's friend."

"Your name?"

"Cupcake Trillin."

"Sorry, I didn't recognize you."

I looked hard at Cupcake. Apparently he was somebody I should recognize, but I didn't.

Owens said, "Mr. and Mrs. Carlyle, would you mind going downtown to the Ringling office and talking there? It'll be more comfortable than standing out in the yard."

For a minute there was a discussion of who would ride in which car, since Zack's car only held two people, with a final decision that Cupcake would ride with Sergeant Owens to the station and wait.

Owens said, "I have to talk to the deputies inside for a minute, and then I'll lead you folks to the station. Dixie, don't leave. I want to talk to you, too."

He meant for me to hang around in the yard until he was ready for me. Former deputies don't get invited to sit in chairs and drink coffee at the sheriff's office. We get interviewed in driveways, on sidewalks, and in the drive-through lane at Taco Bell.

I didn't look forward to being interviewed anywhere. There were too many weird things going on, too many knotted personal relationships, too much sadness.

# 19

Sergeant Owens went into the house, leaving me and Cupcake to watch Zack guide Ruby across the street and help her into his car.

Cupcake said, "You know what's going on here?"

Maybe it was because he was so big, or maybe it was his sweet smile, but I trusted Cupcake.

I said, "I know Ruby is supposed to testify in Myra Kreigle's trial. I know her testimony will send Myra to prison for a long time. I know Myra will go to any lengths to keep that testimony out of court."

Cupcake exhaled, a sigh that came out like a warm wind. "That's what I'm thinking too. That old witch had somebody take that baby to shut Ruby up."

"I think I know who took her. A man named Vern. He grabbed me yesterday and took me to Kantor Tucker. He thought I was Ruby."

Cupcake studied me. "You do look like Ruby."

"Ruby and I thought that would be the end of it. We never dreamed they'd get to her through Opal."

"She should have been with Zack. He's her husband. He should have been watching over her."

"Ruby says Zack believes she tricked him. Is that true?"

He sighed again. "I don't know if that boy knows what he believes anymore. His dad has him all twisted up. He feeds him a lot of crap about how Ruby can't be trusted and how she's a two-timing slut, but it's not true. Ruby's a good girl. She got in with the wrong people, but she didn't know what they were until it was too late."

Sergeant Owens came out the front door, and Cupcake hurried to dig a crumpled card from his pants pocket and hand it to me. "We need to help those kids."

I didn't know if he meant Ruby and Zack or the underprivileged kids he and Zack wanted to help.

Sergeant Owens and I watched Cupcake lumber across the yard to the sheriff's car and crawl into the passenger seat. I sneaked a look at his card but all it said was *Cupcake Trillin*, with a phone number.

Owens said, "You know who that is?"

Without giving me a chance to admit I didn't, he said, "Inside linebacker for the Bucs. He's like a granite mountain."

"Hunh." Being more or less sports illiterate, I didn't know what an inside linebacker was, but I tried to look as if I did.

Owens said, "What do you know about Ruby Carlyle?"

"She used to work for Myra Kreigle, and she's a witness in Myra's trial."

"Okay."

"Ruby's job was to lure rich men into Myra's Ponzi

scheme. That's how she met Zack Carlyle. They were married about eighteen months ago. He and some other athletes had started a foundation to help needy kids. Thanks to Ruby's influence, the foundation invested heavily in Myra Kreigle's phony REIT. I'm not sure how much Ruby knew of what was really going on, but Myra promised her Zack wouldn't lose any money. He lost it all, and now he believes Ruby was as guilty as Myra. Thinks she married him for his money."

Owens raised a bony finger and scratched his cheek a few times, as if he were tabulating suspects.

"Dixie, from what you've seen, do you think there's any chance the mother could be involved in the baby's disappearance? Maybe she's trying to get attention from Zack Carlyle, or maybe she's planning to claim she's too distraught to testify in the Kreigle trial? Maybe this whole thing is a scam, like Kreigle's Ponzi deal. Wouldn't be the first time she's put on a phony act."

He sounded like Zack's father, which made me snap at him. "I haven't seen anything that would make me think that."

That was the absolute truth. I had not seen a thing to make me believe Ruby would engineer a fake kidnapping of her baby. But a good actor can fool anybody, including police officers, judges, juries, and me. Ruby was a good actress, good enough to make old rich men feel young and virile in her presence, good enough to cause them to invest millions of dollars in a phony real estate investment trust. She might have fooled me too, but I didn't believe her love for Opal was faked.

I said, "Yesterday morning a man named Vern Brogher

mistook me for Ruby and strong-armed me into his limo. He took me to see a man named Kantor Tucker. He's the man who put up two million dollars' bond for Myra Kreigle. He has a place out east of Seventy-five where people have airstrips alongside their driveways. When Tucker saw that I wasn't Ruby, he sent Vern away. Vern took me to a Friendly's and put me out. Ruby said Vern was Tucker's muscle, and that he also worked for Myra. Vern may have taken Ruby's baby."

"What about the obese cleaning woman?"

An edge to his voice made me think he was suspicious of the story of the cleaning woman.

I said, "There really is a cleaning woman, and she was truly upset when she saw Opal. And it's true that the women who work with her say she lost a baby a few weeks ago, and that her boyfriend left her."

"But you think the kidnapper may be that Vern guy?"

In my memory, I heard Ruby talking about Tuck shoving a man out of his plane over the Gulf. And I heard Tucker's threatening voice say that Opal could become shark food. Ruby was afraid to accuse Vern because she was afraid Tuck and Myra would kill Opal if she did. I was afraid of that too.

I said, "All I know is that Myra Kreigle's trial begins Monday, and if Ruby testifies about what Myra did with the money she took from people, Myra may spend the rest of her life in jail. If Ruby thought Vern had kidnapped her baby to keep her quiet, she might decide not to tell what she knows. Myra would get a shorter prison sentence, and the stolen money would still be there waiting when she got out."

He looked skeptical, and I didn't blame him. A criminal investigation can't run on speculation and vague hunches.

"That's an interesting theory, Dixie. You have anything except intuition to back it up?"

I clenched my jaws on words that begged to be said: *I heard Tucker tell Ruby that Opal might become shark food if Ruby said bad things about her friends.* I had no right to say those words. Like Ruby, I had to choose between telling the truth and saving Opal's life.

Owens said, "We'll put out an Amber Alert right away, and we'll notify public transportation services to be on the lookout for an obese Caucasian woman with a four-month-old baby."

"That ought to narrow down the field."

Ignoring the sarcasm, he gave me a half salute and strode off to join Cupcake in the car. Dully, I watched them drive away, watched Zack and Ruby pull in behind to follow them to the sheriff's office.

Except for a lone deputy car, my Bronco was the only vehicle left. Firefighters were putting equipment back into their trucks and driving away. Across the street, neighbors were retrieving their quilts and pillows from the grass and returning to their own homes.

The fire marshall's investigating team hadn't yet arrived, and I knew the deputy inside was mostly biding time until they showed up. I had no reason to stay, but I couldn't make my feet move. I felt as if I were an impostor in my own body, somebody who looked like me and talked like me but was a total stranger to me. When I'd agreed with Ruby that the cleaning woman might have kidnapped Opal, I had helped implicate an innocent woman in a crime. It didn't help that I knew she would be found innocent. I had violated every principle I held dear.

But I wanted to save Opal, and I believed Tucker could get away with murdering a baby without ever being called to account for it. He was that powerful, he was that amoral. If he and Myra were accused, he might dispose of Opal just to be rid of the evidence.

The sun was mid-heaven now, way past my breakfast time. But I was too grimy and sad to eat. The only thing I could do was go to my apartment, my quiet refuge away from insanity and greed, away from twisted people who could justify stealing a baby in order to force its mother to lie to a jury.

A car door slammed shut in Myra's driveway, and I turned to see a black Mercedes back to the street and drive away. Seconds later, a red BMW backed rapidly from Myra's garage to the street, it turned with squealing brakes, and roared away. Myra and Tucker had both left her house.

I turned and looked at Myra's house. The young woman I'd seen at the window might be in there alone. Or she might have Opal with her. Vern might have come down the side of the vacant house into Mr. Stern's side yard, sneaked into Ruby's bedroom, set the fire, grabbed Opal from her crib, and left the same way he'd come, circling behind Mr. Stern's walled garden to the back of Myra's yard and into her house without anybody seeing him. Opal might have been inside the house while Myra and Tucker talked to Ruby at the front door. If that were true, Opal could be inside Myra's house right that moment, and Myra and Tucker were gone.

The young woman I'd seen at Myra's window had looked gentle and kind. Defenseless, even. I was an ex-deputy. I had gone to police academy. I was not gentle and kind. If that soft young woman was alone in Myra's house with Opal, I could go in and easily take the baby away from her.

After I had the baby, I would call Sergeant Owens and he would make sure the baby was put in a safe place. Ruby would be able to tell the truth, and Myra and Tucker would spend the rest of their lives in prison. Most important of all, Ruby and Opal would be safe.

I didn't see a single flaw in my reasoning. That's how far gone I was.

# 20

A modest corridor of lawn separated Mr. Stern's walled courtyard from Myra Kreigle's driveway. I circled the end of the wall separating the lots and looked down the side of Myra's house. Flower beds ran alongside the house's foundation, and a gravel walk between the beds and the driveway was edged with begonias. The walk led to a side door. That side door beckoned me.

I took the crunching graveled walk to the side door. Anybody watching would have seen me moving at a normal speed, not running like a thief. At the door, my hand tried the doorknob. Myra must have been in too much of a hurry to lock it when she left, because it turned. I pushed the door open and stepped into a spacious laundry room with side-by-side washer and dryer and cupboards above.

I moved into the kitchen where a window above the sink let in midday sunshine. Even gliding through as quickly as I did, I appreciated the way the kitchen managed to look both contemporary and antique. Dark wood floors, granite countertops, glossy dark cabinets that reached to the ceiling, and a pale green stove with French Provincial legs and a hooded top. The stove pretended to be vintage, but was undoubtedly a reproduction that had cost an obscene amount of money. A wide baker's cabinet stood at an angle in a corner, either a genuine antique or a very good reproduction. I doubted that Myra ever pulled out its work table and kneaded dough or rolled pie crusts on it. It was strictly for show, like everything else in Myra's life.

The living room was equally charming, with Oriental rugs and paintings that looked as if a decorator had chosen them to match the color scheme. Staying well back from wide windows veiled in sheer curtains, I took in a ceiling with pecky-cypress beams. The brick on the fireplace looked old. Myra had probably robbed it from some medieval castle.

Scuttling through the living room as fast as I could, I raced through a slew of richly decorated downstairs rooms, then took heart-pine stairs to the second floor. The house was shadowy and quiet, the way an empty house would be. But I didn't believe the house was empty. I believed a young Latin American woman was in it. Perhaps willingly, perhaps as a prisoner.

Careful not to let the soles of my Keds squeak on the wooden floors, I walked as quickly as I could down a central hall with doors on each side, some closed, some open. I sped down the hall looking first into every open door, then retraced my steps to check the rooms with closed doors. It was deathly quiet, and a nugget of doubt began to work its way into my brain. Maybe I'd been wrong, maybe the young woman I'd seen wasn't here.

One closed door led to a bedroom in which a satin dressing gown was tossed over the foot of the bed, and the scent of expensive perfume hung in the air. I guessed it was Myra's, but I didn't take time to investigate. Another door led to a guest room with a king-size bed, gender-free maroon bedspread, a long dresser, and two club chairs. It smelled of furniture polish, and had a private bath with rolled stacks of maroon towels. Another led to a no-frills bedroom with a beige tailored spread on a double bed. The bedspread was rumpled, as if something had been moved around on it, and the wooden floor had the kind of detritus that falls out of opened purses or luggage—tiny shreds of tissue, bits of foil from chewing gum wrappers, a broken rubber band. This bedroom also had a private bath. The towels were white and not as plush as the maroon ones. A damp washcloth had been carefully folded over the lip of the sink.

In my imagination, I saw the young dark-haired woman pack a cheap suitcase she'd laid on the bed, saw her wash her face and hands, saw her take time to fold her washcloth before she hurried from the room. She hadn't had time to smooth the bedspread or pick up what the luggage had shed when she'd opened it.

I had been wrong about the young woman being in the house, and I had to get out before Myra returned. Downstairs, I skittered through the living room and into the kitchen. At the side door, I reached to turn the knob. The crunch of approaching footsteps on the gravel path made me jerk my hand away.

Like a cornered rat, I ran back into the kitchen, my eyes darting back and forth for any hiding spot. The side doorknob rattled, and I dived for the lower doors on the baker's cabinet. The angels that protect idiots must have been with me, because that base section was empty and big enough for me to wedge myself into. I pulled the doors closed and held my breath while footsteps clattered from the laundry room.

Of all the pin-headed, numb-nutted, dumb-assed things I'd ever done, this one was the star on the tree. My chin dug into my knees, my fingers gripped my tight-folded legs, and I didn't dare take a good breath for fear the person who'd just come in would hear me. If I sneezed or coughed, I was done for.

Four feet away from my hiding place, Myra's voice said, "Tuck? Where are you? Why aren't you answering your cell?"

She waited a beat and then grew more shrill. "Vern scared Angelina and she ran away. Went out on the highway and some woman picked her up and brought her to a bodega on Clark Road. You have to drive her back there. Call me as soon as you get this."

A softer voice said, "I will not stay in house with that man." She spoke with an accent, and with a Latin rhythm.

With daggers in every word, Myra said, "Angelina, do you remember what I told you would happen to your mother if you broke your promise?"

"That man say if I don't do what he wants, he will give me to those alligators. Big alligators, both sides of the road."

Myra muttered, "Son of a bitch."

A cell phone beeped, and Myra snarled an answer. "Tuck, you've got to take control of that damned man! He stayed in the house with Angelina and threatened her."

A pause, and then, "What do you mean, you can't take her back? You have to! I can't take the time to drive forty miles to that house! I have a million things to do before the trial starts."

Another pause, and Myra made a groaning sound of pure fury. I imagined she had bared her teeth.

Silence stretched, and Myra heaved an exaggerated sigh. "All right, I'll drive her! But you have to take care of Vern!"

Another silence. "Okay. Okay. When your meeting is over, call me."

She must have closed her phone, because her next words were to Angelina. "Mr. Tucker says for you to be a good girl and keep your promise so nothing bad will happen to your mother. I'll drive you back to the house, and you must not leave again."

"I not stay in house with that man."

"Mr. Tucker promises the man won't bother you again."

Angelina made mumbling noises of reluctant assent.

Cowering in my tight quarters, I listened to Myra's high heels clicking to the side door along with Angelina's soft padding. The door opened and closed.

I waited until I was sure they weren't coming back, then eased my cramped self out of the baker's cabinet and limped to the side door. When I stuck my head out, I didn't see anybody. I slipped out the door, pulled it closed, and sauntered to the Bronco as nonchalantly as I could manage. The deputy's car was still at the curb. The neighborhood looked the same. The only thing that had changed was me.

In the Bronco, a surge of adrenaline caused me to grip

the steering wheel and tremble for a while. When the shakes passed, I started the motor and drove away in a state of euphoric frustration. I had learned some valuable information, but I wasn't sure what it was.

Neither Myra nor Angelina had mentioned a baby. But I would have bet my entire collection of white Keds that Vern had taken Opal and Angelina to a house somewhere forty miles away where Vern had scared Angelina so much she'd run away. If I was right, she had left Opal alone with Vern.

With my head pounding from exhaustion, stress, and hunger, I headed home, where the carport looked bleakly empty and the shorebirds walking along the edge of the surf seemed sad and dispirited. In my bathroom, I was shocked when I saw my reflection in the mirror. My skin was streaked with a greasy film of gray smoke, my eyes were red-rimmed and pink-veined, and my hair clung to my scalp in heavy dull strands. I not only felt like hell, I looked like hell.

Peeling off my smoke-stinking clothes, I stuffed them in the washer. Cupcake's wrinkled card fluttered to the floor, and I retrieved it and put it in my bag. Just knowing it had been in Cupcake's big warm hand gave the card a peculiar kind of power I wanted to hold on to.

As I got into a hot shower, I heard my cell phone's distinctive ring reserved for Michael, Paco, or Guidry. I let it ring. I was too tired and too nasty to talk to anybody. As blessed hot water sluiced over my skin and hair and washed away the odor and fatigue, I realized that I was still shaking. Fine tremors seemed to be emanating from my bones, traveling through my flesh and jittering my skin in a combination of adrenaline, exhaustion, fear, and shame.

When I was sure I was free of the stench and grime from smoke, I stepped out of the shower, toweled off, and pulled a shaky comb through my hair. Walking like a feeble old woman, I shuffled to my bed and crawled under the covers, already halfway into the oblivion of sleep.

I dreamed I was in some cavernous place where shadowy forms moved around me. I knew they carried important information, but none of them would come close so I could find out what it was. When I chased them, they dissolved, and when I stood still and begged them to come to me, they turned into hard boulders that couldn't move.

A banging at my french doors pulled me from the dream. Guidry was on the porch yelling my name. I groaned. There are times in a relationship when you are ecstatic to see the other person, and there are times when you just want to be left the hell alone.

Louder, Guidry yelled, "Dixie?"

I groaned again and slid out of bed. I was halfway to the door when I remembered I was stark naked, so I detoured to the closet and grabbed a sleepshirt. Not that Guidry hadn't seen me naked before, but answering the door wearing nothing but skin seemed just wrong. Decently covered, I yanked open the french doors. In the next instant, Guidry was holding me close and I was blubbering all over his nice linen jacket.

He said, "Owens called me and told me about the fire."

I sobbed, "They took Opal."

"The baby?"

I rubbed my face up and down against his chest. "Uh-huh."

"Who? Who took her?"

I opened my mouth to answer him, and the little male secretary in my brain who zips around opening file drawers to retrieve information when I need it came to a screeching halt. Whirling to a specific filing cabinet, he whipped out a file marked "Officers of the Law Are Required to Report All Crimes of Which They Have Knowledge."

Once again, I was faced with the partnered-person's dilemma. I had good reason to believe that Vern had taken Opal and put her in a house forty miles away. But I had to choose between gut instinct, which was to share my awful secret with Guidry, and the knowledge that his integrity as an officer of the law would compel him to take actions that might lead to Opal's death.

Pulling away from him, I wiped away tears with both hands. It gave me an excuse not to look up at Guidry.

"It may have been Vern. Or it could have been a cleaning woman who was at the Stern house yesterday."

My little brain secretary smiled and replaced the file.

"Owens said the fire was arson."

"That's what Michael said, too. He saved Cheddar."

"Cheddar?"

"Mr. Stern's cat. Cheddar was in the bedroom with Opal, and he hid under the bed. Michael found him and brought him out to the EMTs and they gave him oxygen. He's at the animal hospital now, but they think he's going to be okay."

Guidry smoothed my damp hair back from my forehead. "What about you? Are you going to be okay?"

I burst into sobs again. Stood there and bawled like a two-year-old. "I'm hungry, and Michael's at the firehouse and I don't have anything to eat."

Guidry chuckled and pulled me into his arms again. "Tell you what, I'll cook dinner for you tonight at my place."

I wailed, "I'm not crying because I'm hungry."

"I know."

"I didn't know you could cook."

"You still don't. It's only a theory."

He squeezed me in a hug, kissed the top of my head, and released me. "You need to sleep. I'll see you tonight."

Crying, hiccuping, and sniffling, I watched him walk across my porch. I watched him go down the stairs until his head disappeared from view. Then I pulled the french doors closed, pushed the button to lower the folding metal hurricane shutters, and shuffled back to bed, sobbing all the way. I was still crying when I fell asleep. Maybe I even cried while I slept.

# 21

My nap lasted only about fifteen minutes, way too short, and I woke feeling headachy and depressed. The headache was a no-food-since-last-night dullness. The depression was a crushing weight made from worry about what was happening to Opal, wondering where Vern had taken Opal, and guilt from being partially responsible for the sheriff's office including in its list of suspects an innocent cleaning woman already torn by grief over losing a baby.

I padded to the kitchen and put on water for tea. I thought about going downstairs to Michael's kitchen and raiding his refrigerator, but I couldn't dredge up energy for more than pouring water over tea bags. While I drank a cup of under-brewed tea, I wondered how long it would take Sergeant Owens to remove the cleaning woman from his suspects.

When I couldn't stand it any more, I pulled out my cellphone and dialed his number. It was engraved in my memory from my days as a deputy.

When Sergeant Owens answered, I said, "This is Dixie. I just wondered if you'd got any leads about the kidnapped baby."

He sounded surprised. Not at my curiosity, but that I'd called him.

Carefully, as if he didn't want to hurt my feelings, Owens said, "I know you're concerned about the baby, Dixie. We all are. But it may take time to find her. We've put out an Amber Alert, and we have people searching the neighborhood. We also have the cleaning woman's full name. Doreen Antone. We've tracked down her address, but nobody's home and her car's gone. We've talked to Doreen's boyfriend, and he said she might have gone to her sister's in Alabama. He's thick as a board, doesn't know where the sister lives, like what town, but he knows Doreen is from Alabama and that she has a sister there. We've alerted airports and bus stations and put out an APB to be on the lookout for an overweight young Caucasian woman with a four-month-old baby. We're checking high school records, DMV records, everything we can. We'll find her."

My chest felt as if a trapped eagle were inside flapping its wings against my heart in a desperate search for truth that would lead to freedom. But the terrible truth was that Myra and Tucker had more money than all the law enforcement agencies in the country. Money is power, and Myra and Tucker were ruthless in their use of it. If I told Sergeant Owens that following Doreen Antone was a useless expenditure of department energy and money, I'd have to tell him the truth about Opal being held in a house forty miles away. That could lead to Tucker learning he was a suspect. If he did, Opal could be dead and disposed of in an hour. I couldn't jeopardize Opal's safety by telling Owens the truth. Like Ruby, I had to swallow my honor and accept the unacceptable.

I thanked Owens, apologized for taking his time, and rang off with more worry and remorse than I'd felt before I called. Knowing about Ruby's tacit agreement with Tucker and Myra had given me the ability to see the future with an awful clarity. At Myra's trial, Ruby wouldn't remember a single offshore account where Myra had stashed millions in stolen money. In exchange, Kantor Tucker would keep his part of the agreement and fly Opal and Angelina to another part of the country where they would be discreetly installed in a nice house and given a plausible cover story. Angelina would be supplied with all the papers necessary to pose as Opal's mother, and nobody would suspect that Opal had been kidnapped. In ten years or fifteen or twenty, whenever Myra was released from prison, she and Tucker would collect the offshore accounts. If Ruby was out of jail by that time, they might permit her to be reunited with Opal, but Opal's love and allegiance would be to the woman who had raised her.

Now here's the thing about secrets: Like the Big Bad Wolf, secrets have big jagged teeth and strong jaws. Kept inside, they use their sharp teeth to tear off big chunks of your tender innards, gnashing your flesh in their spring-trap jaws and ripping you to shreds. Secrets have to be told to *somebody*, just not to somebody who will repeat them or who will be personally affected by them. Somebody like a trusted psychotherapist, maybe, or a spiritual guide. I didn't know any psychotherapists or spiritual guides, but I knew Cora Mathers, and I felt a sudden urge to get to her as fast as possible. In a feverish rush, I pulled on clothes, grabbed my keys and bag, and hurried out my front door.

I took the north bridge to Tamiami Trail, followed it around the marina where tall sailboats were anchored, and then a few blocks to Bayfront Village, an upscale retirement condo on the bay. A uniformed parking attendant rushed out to open my Bronco's door, and double glass doors sighed open to let me pass into the big lobby. Handsome elderly people stood around in groups making dates to play tennis or golf or to go to the opera or the museum or a movie. I don't know why it is, but rich old people seem to have more fun than young people, rich or poor. Maybe it's because old people who are rich had to be luckier or smarter than other people to get rich in the first place, so they use the same luck and smarts to enjoy old age.

I headed for the elevators, and from her place behind a big French provincial desk, the concierge waved and picked up her house phone to let Cora know I was coming. She knew that Cora always wanted to see me, so I didn't have to wait for permission.

Cora is in her late eighties, but she's the youngest person I know. Cora and her granddaughter started out poor, but her granddaughter made a lot of money in ways that Cora has never suspected, and she bought Cora a posh apartment in the Bayfront Village. The granddaughter was murdered while she was a client of mine a few years back, and Cora and I became close friends. She's not at all like my own grandmother was, but she has sort of taken her place. I'm not at all like her granddaughter either, but in many ways I've taken her place. Which I guess proves that friendships don't depend on any of the things we think they do, they just happen when two people like each other a lot.

On the sixth floor, Cora's door was already open and she had stuck her head out to watch for me. Cora is roughly the size of an undernourished middle-school child, with thin freckled arms and legs and white hair so thin and wispy her pink scalp shines through. When she saw me step out of the elevator, she waved her entire arm up and down like a highway flagman, as if she thought I wouldn't know which door was hers if she didn't signal.

Before I got to the door, she said, "You knew I was baking bread, didn't you? I'll bet you smelled it all the way across town."

I could smell it now, and the scent drew me forward like the odor of cream to a kitten. Cora has an old bread-making machine that was a gift from her granddaughter, and by a secret recipe that she won't divulge, she makes decadent chocolate bread in it.

I gave Cora a hug—carefully, because I'm always afraid I'll crush her—and followed her into her pink and turquoise apartment. It's a lovely apartment, pink marble floors, paler pink walls, turquoise and rose linen covers on sofa and chairs, and a terrace beyond a glass wall through which she has a magnificent view of the bay.

The odor of hot chocolate bread made me walk with lifted nose like a hound first getting a scent of something to chase.

Cora said, "I just took it out, so it's piping hot."

Habit made Cora take a seat at a small skirted table between the living area and a tiny one-person kitchen while I assembled our tea tray. Cora's teakettle is always on, so it only took a minute to pour hot water over tea bags in a Brown Betty pot, get cups and saucers from the cupboard, butter from the refrigerator, and add the hot round loaf of chocolate bread. I put the tray on the table and took the other chair. Cora watched me lay everything out and pour two cups of tea.

We each tore off two fist-sized hunks of bread from the loaf—Cora insists that it can't be sliced like ordinary bread—and slathered them with butter. Cora's chocolate bread is dark, dense, and studded with morsels of semi-sweet chocolate that have not fully melted but instead gently ooze from their centers. Angels in heaven probably have Cora's chocolate bread with tea every afternoon. If God's on their good side, they may invite him to join them. I ate half my chunk before I said a word. Partly because it was so good, and partly because I couldn't get the words out.

Cora said, "You look like you've been wrung dry. What's wrong?"

I don't know how she does it, but she always knows.

I sipped tea and put my cup back in its saucer. "A baby I know has been kidnapped. She's about four months old. Her name is Opal, and she's beautiful. I'm sure I know who took her, but if I tell, it could cause her to be killed."

Cora tilted her head toward the light coming in from the glass sliders at the back of her living room so that the fine lines that etched her skin seemed to shimmer.

"You're sure you know?"

I took a bite of bread and chewed while I tried to figure out a way to tell Cora how I knew that Myra and
Tucker had sent Vern to kidnap Opal.

I said, "It's too complicated to go into all the details,
but I overheard a phone conversation. There's a man and
woman who hired another man to take the baby. They did
it because the baby's mother knows things about them
that can get them sent to prison for a long time. If she
keeps quiet, they'll take good care of her baby, but she'll
go to prison. If she tells what she knows, she won't go to
prison, but they'll kill her baby."

Cora laced her fingers together on the table. "It would
take a very low person to kill a baby."

"They're that low. They're about as low as a human being can get."

"You don't think you might have misunderstood what
you heard?"

I shook my head. "I heard enough to convince me. The
baby's mother has known them a long time and she says
the man has flown his plane out over the Gulf and shoved
people out. She thinks he'll do that to the baby if she
talks."

"My goodness."

"I don't know what to do. I'm afraid to tell what I know,
and afraid not to tell."

She took a sip of tea, her hooded blue eyes watching
me.

She said, "Losing a baby is the worst thing that can
ever happen to a person. You don't ever get over it. You
can think you've moved away from the hurt, but every

time you hear about some other baby being lost, you feel like it's happening to you all over again."

My breath caught in my chest as if a hand had grabbed my throat, and in the next instant my face was buried in my hands and I was sobbing again, not about Opal but because my baby had been crushed to death in an insane accident in a supermarket parking lot. Cora did not get up and comfort me. She was too smart for that. She waited me out. And because I knew she was strong enough to wait me out, I didn't try to dam my flood of tears but let them flow until they slowed to a trickle and stopped.

When I took my hands from my face, Cora handed me a stack of paper napkins. I mopped my cheeks and gave her a tremulous smile. "I didn't expect to do that."

She said, "Oh, you'll always do that. It'll catch you when you're not even thinking about your child. It's been over forty years since my daughter died and left me her baby to raise, but sometimes it hits me all over again that she's gone, and I'm just laid low. I don't guess it will ever stop, that awful pain. It just goes into hiding for long stretches."

I said, "The baby's mother is very young, and she already has a lot of heartache, and now this goon has kidnapped her baby. It's just not fair."

"I don't know why people are always surprised that life isn't fair. It never has been, never will be. You can't do anything about that."

"I guess not."

Cora said, "Well, you have to find that baby and bring her home. Her mother's not going to be able to help you much. Women aren't much good at getting things done when they're scared and grieving. Men are better at that.

Seems like they can turn all their grief into action. Go bomb something, shoot somebody, start a fistfight, bust up a saloon. Half the time they make it worse, but at least they can move. At least they can do *something*."

I said, "The baby's father is a race car driver."

Cora's pale blue eyes lit with some old memory. "Race car drivers are good at taking action. They're good at breaking hearts, too. If I was you, I'd get the dad to help you get that baby back. See if he's got the gumption to do something besides break a woman's heart."

From the acid in her voice, I thought it was a safe guess that Cora's heart had once been broken by a race car driver.

I said, "I don't know the father very well."

She shrugged. "You can fix that."

As usual, Cora had oversimplified a complex situation that she knew nothing about. But for some fool reason I felt as if a huge load had been lifted from me. I even felt as if she'd given me a solution of sorts. All I had to do was figure out how to put it into action.

I put away our tea things and kissed the top of Cora's feathery head.

I said, "Thank you. For the bread, for the tea, for listening to me."

She patted my hand. "You're a good girl, Dixie. You just have to stay strong."

As I rode down in the elevator, I told myself Cora was absolutely right. I needed to stay strong. And maybe, just maybe, Zack Carlyle was the person who would help me find Opal.

Before the elevator came to a stop on the lobby level, I

had pulled out Cupcake's card. By the time the valet brought my car to me, I had called Cupcake and asked to meet with him. He seemed to have been expecting my call. We agreed to meet in thirty minutes at the Daiquiri Deck on Siesta Key. When I rang off, I almost felt as if I'd accomplished something.

# 22

A favorite meeting place for both locals and tourists, the Daiquiri Deck is a raised veranda restaurant on Ocean Boulevard. Partly a young people's pick-up joint, partly a viewing platform to watch passing foot traffic, and partly just a place to get tasty food and drinks, the Deck is the spot where everybody who comes to the Key eventually ends up.

I took an umbrella table where I could watch for Cupcake, ordered an iced tea, and scanned the menu while I waited. Cora's chocolate bread had helped, but I needed more food in me before I left for afternoon pet rounds. I asked for an order of buffalo shrimp with bleu cheese sauce, and had just dunked a crispy fried shrimp into a bowl of sauce when Cupcake appeared at the top of the steps. Zack was with him, looking suspicious and unhappy.

I waved at them and took a bit of pleasure from the way men's heads turned to watch them walk to me. I had been invisible before, but now every male on the Deck looked at me with new appreciation. Not because I had suddenly become a guy magnet, but because I knew Zack and Cupcake. One or two men actually stopped Cupcake and Zack to ask for autographs, and the others gazed at them with such shining eyes you would have thought the hottest chick on the planet had arrived.

Cupcake and Zack pulled out chairs and sat down without speaking to me. Not in an unfriendly way, just all business. Cupcake eyed my buffalo shrimp and beckoned to a waitress. "Bring two more orders of that, and a Corona on draft. Zack, what do you want?"

Zack looked startled. "Um, I'll have a Corona too."

The waitress scurried away, and Cupcake watched me lay a shrimp tail on my plate.

"You don't eat the tails?"

"I just use the tails as handles."

"Where I come from, people think the tails are the best part."

I opened my mouth to ask him where that might be, but Zack interrupted us.

"Why did you call?"

He sounded like a man who'd been tricked into making an appearance before, only to discover that somebody had merely wanted to be seen with him.

I said, "Zack, I just want to help you find Opal."

Zack fell silent, as if listening to some other voices inside his own head. I guessed some of the voices belonged to his father. A beat passed, and he spoke as if he'd been contemplating speech for a long time.

"It's hard to know what to do, you know? When to give a woman what she wants, and when to be a man and hang tough."

Cupcake visibly tensed.

I said, "Maybe being a man *is* giving a woman what she wants."

Zack moved his lower jaw back and forth as if he needed to line up his teeth.

"Before she died, my mom had to prop her head up with her hand. For two or three years she went around with one hand on the back of her head holding it up. She even drove like that. You'd see her going past, one hand on the steering wheel and one hand holding up her head." He stared into the hot sky. "My dad didn't do a thing to stop her. Not one thing."

"Was there a medical problem that made your mother's neck weak?"

"Nah, she just wanted Dad's attention."

He seemed to be comparing himself to the kind of husband his father had been and finding himself superior. I wondered if he thought Ruby's involvement with Myra had been like his mother's weak neck. Maybe he believed he'd been more of a man because he'd turned against Ruby because she'd worked for Myra.

His lips tightened into a mirthless smile. "The Thanksgiving before she died, she asked Dad if he couldn't say something nice about the big dinner she'd cooked. He said he didn't intend to thank her just for doing her job."

It occurred to me that he was a younger version of Mr. Stern, which was probably why Ruby had been drawn to him. She was familiar with men who couldn't show emotion or give affection.

I said, "Every woman in the world wants attention and praise from her husband, Zack. And by the way, Ruby didn't marry you for your money. She truly loved you."

Zack looked shocked and suspicious, as if he'd caught me trying to put one over on him.

Cupcake heaved a sigh that seemed to have a lot of history with Zack's distrust of women behind it. "When you called, you said you had information. What is it?"

"I think I know who took Opal. And I think we can put our heads together and figure out where she is."

Zack's blue-purple eyes almost disappeared in a skeptical squint. "If you know something, you should tell the cops."

"I'm afraid telling what I know could make matters worse."

I wiped my shrimpy hands on a napkin and leaned forward. I gave them a quick rundown of how Vern had kidnapped me the day before and taken me to Kantor Tucker's place. I told them I believed Myra had seen me in Mr. Stern's courtyard and ordered Vern to grab me. I told them about the young woman I'd seen at Myra's window.

The waitress came bearing beer and two orders of buffalo shrimp. She put a plate in front of each man, but Zack pushed his across the table to Cupcake. Deftly, Cupcake transferred all the shrimp to one plate and handed the empty to the waitress.

As soon as she left us, Cupcake circled a finger the size of a bratwurst for me to go on with my story.

"This morning, after everybody left Mr. Stern's house, I saw both Tucker and Myra leave. I thought the young woman might be in the house with Opal. It was stupid, I know, but I went into Myra's house looking for Opal."

Zack looked disapproving, Cupcake put a whole shrimp in his mouth and beamed at me.

Zack said, "So you like to involve yourself in the affairs of well-known people, is that it? Think you'd like to see your name in the newspaper?"

I felt heat rising to my face. "My name has been in the newspaper several times, Zack, and I hated it. Once was when my husband and child were killed. I know the pain of losing a child, and I hope you and Ruby never feel that pain."

Zack looked chastened.

I said, "Just for the record, I was a deputy for several years."

Cupcake raised a plate-sized hand. "Dixie, there's something you should know too, just for the record. The arson investigators found some nitrous oxide canisters in the bedroom where the fire was. They questioned Zack about them."

"I don't understand."

Zack's voice was bitter. "Pro Modified racers use nitrous oxide to supercharge their engines. I don't do Pro Modified racing, I'm Pro Stock, but whoever started that fire tried to implicate me with those canisters."

I said, "There was a weird sweet smell along with the smoke."

"That would have been the nitrous oxide. It's not flammable itself, but it intensifies fire."

"I don't imagine the kind of people who kidnap babies and set fire to their bedrooms would get all moral when it came to leaving false evidence behind."

"You're right. Sorry to act like an ass. Go on with your story."

I could see why Ruby had fallen for him. He had a problem with expressing emotion, but he made up for it with integrity.

I said, "I went all through Myra's house, but it was empty. I can't be sure, but it looked like somebody had packed a suitcase in one of the bedrooms. Before I could leave, Myra came home with a young Hispanic woman named Angelina. I hid, and I heard enough to know that Angelina had run away from a house where Vern had taken her. He had frightened her so badly that she'd gone out on a highway where a woman picked her up and took her to a bodega on Clark Road. She had called Myra to come get her. Myra was furious at her, and called Tucker to tell him he had to drive Angelina back to where she'd been. She got even more furious when Tucker told her she'd have to do it herself. She said she didn't have time to drive forty miles to deliver Angelina. She had no choice, though, so she promised Angelina that Vern wouldn't bother her again, and they left. That's where Opal is, forty miles away."

Both men stared at me.

Cupcake said, "Forty miles in which direction? In which house?"

Zack said, "This isn't information, it's gossip."

I said, "Think about it. Angelina said there were lots of alligators on the road, on both sides."

Dryly, Cupcake said, "Well, that narrows it down to about every road in Florida."

"Not really. She sounded like the alligators were very close to the road, the way they are along Highway Seventy-two where it goes through Myakka State Park. The alligators along that stretch of road are huge. They'd scare anybody walking along the shoulder."

Cupcake dipped two shrimp at one time into runny bleu cheese. "I don't think there *is* a shoulder on that stretch."

"That's what I'm talking about."

Zack said, "Have you told this to the officer handling the investigation?"

I studied his face, looking for a sign that would tell me he had the imagination to think in a non-linear, non-rote, non-lockstep way. The only thing I saw was a young man dazed by shock and misery.

I said, "If either of you repeat what I'm going to tell you, I'll deny that I ever said it."

Their necks straightened and their eyes widened. Cupcake even stopped eating.

"You know when Myra and Tucker spoke to Ruby this morning? And how Ruby told you she'd been wrong to think Myra had anything to do with the kidnapping? Well, she lied. I heard what Myra and Tucker said to her. They didn't exactly spell it out, but they made it plain that Opal would be kept safe if Ruby zipped her lips at Myra's trial. But if Ruby tells the truth about where Myra put all the money she stole from investors, Opal will be thrown to sharks."

A spasm of pain flickered across Zack's face. He took a long, shuddering breath, his jaws clamped together so hard that his lean cheek muscles quivered.

I said, "If this were a TV show, I'd go tell the investigators and they'd arrest Myra and Tucker, find Opal, and bring her home. But this is the real world, and Tucker is richer than the state of Florida. He probably owns a crooked cop in every county. The minute Tucker becomes a person of interest in Opal's disappearance, one of his informers will call him and warn him. He could dispose of Opal's little body in a million different ways, one of which could be tossing her to alligators in one of those swamps in Myakka Park."

Zack said, "What do you have in mind?"

"First, we have to find out where they're hiding her. Then we have to go in and get her."

A look passed between Cupcake and Zack, one of those *Are-you-thinking-what-I'm-thinking?* looks that old friends do.

Cupcake said, "Chainsaw's."

Zack nodded. "If anywhere, that would be the place."

While I tried to figure out what the heck they were talking about, Zack seemed to go inside himself and wrestle with an inner demon. After a long moment, he looked from Cupcake to me with a stern young face. "Ordinarily, I'd say we had to play it by the book, not play vigilante and take the law into our own hands. But not this time. This time my baby's life is on the line, not some principle."

Cupcake gave Zack a dimpled smile. "Atta boy."

I said, "Who's Chainsaw?"

Cupcake said, "It's a what, not a who. Dive on the edge of Bradenton where lowlifes like baby-kidnappers hang out. Somebody there may know something."

In one fluid motion, Zack stood up and tossed money on the table. "Let's go."

I said, "I'll follow you." No way in hell was I going to let them go without me.

Zack was moving toward the steps to the sidewalk as if the decision to act had galvanized him. Cupcake and I hurried after him.

Cupcake said, "You got a cap or something? Somebody in that place might recognize you."

I had already had the same thought. If Vern or one of the guys who'd kidnapped me hung out at the bar, they'd spot me at once.

I said, "It's in my truck. Also some dark shades."

On the sidewalk, Zack and Cupcake rushed to Zack's convertible and I loped off to my Bronco. Zack waited to pull away from the curb until there was a gap in traffic big enough to let me swing into the street behind him. You can tell a lot about a person by the way they handle being the lead car in a two-car convoy. Whether they're thoughtless or aware, whether they're able to gauge their speed so both cars end up on the same side of a red traffic light, whether they weave in and out of traffic or stay in the same lane. Zack was a good leader. My respect for him was climbing, but I still wished he would be his own man and not let his father push him around.

Chainsaw's turned out to be a squat building in one of Florida's few remaining old fishing villages on Cortez Road, a narrow street connecting Anna Maria Island to the mainland. Grill net bans have mostly put commercial fishermen out of business, but nostalgia and stubbornness have kept a few areas free of high-rises and hotels. Chainsaw's was in one of those moldy places. It sat at one end of an almost abandoned strip center. A Goodwill store was at the other end.

Neither looked as if they were frequented by people living the good life.

# 23

I parked next to Zack's car in an odd-shaped graveled lot full of potholes deep enough to lose a child in. I rummaged in the Bronco's glove box and dragged out an old black cap with a big bill and a fishing lure embroidered on the front. It had originally belonged to Michael, and it had been in my car long enough to acquire a patina of aged dust. With my ponytail coiled under it and the cap pulled low over a big pair of dark glasses, I felt sufficiently disguised to pass under Vern's nose without being recognized.

Crossing the uneven lot toward Chainsaw's entrance felt as distasteful and dangerous as slogging across the river Styx. To add to the feeling, Chainsaw's entrance was flanked by a row of humanoid figures crudely carved from driftwood. Every head was identical, with round maniacal eyes like sixteenth-century gargoyles. A tattoo parlor next door to Chainsaw's had a big red NO DRUNKS! sign on the front door, but the sign looked as if it was accustomed to being ignored.

Inside, it was so dark that we had to wait a moment to let our eyes get accustomed to the change from bright sunshine. Considering the early afternoon hour, the place was surprisingly crowded. Shadowy masculine figures that looked a lot like the driftwood carvings slumped on bar stools, other men hunched over tables centered by dim lights inside thick red shades. A few heads turned to look our way, but mostly the men seemed too absorbed in their own bored resentment. Florida fishermen have long memories, and they'll never reconcile to being ruined to further tourism and development.

When we could see, we followed a waitress way too old for the loose tank top that revealed sagging bare breasts in front and a mermaid tattooed across her back. She showed us to a table, took our orders, and weaved her way through tables and drunks coming from the men's room. We sat back and scanned the room, not certain who we were looking for, but hoping we would recognize him if he was there. The men at the bar were silent, drinking bottled beer and staring at the wall covered by faded photographs of fishermen and their boats.

To one side of us, a drunken middle-aged man and woman were deep into sloppy pre-coital grins and slurred innuendos they believed were clever. He probably had a wife somewhere at work, but for the moment he was caught in the illusion of being free and desirable. They pushed back their chairs and left as the waitress brought our beers.

With practiced disdain, she watched the couple maneuver through the door with their arms around each other's waists. "Between you and me, that woman's days for making money with her body should have ended about ten years ago. Now she's got it all held together with them elastic underthings, those whatcha-call-'em, Stanks."

I said, "Spanx."

She set our beers down with sharp clicks.

"You go around pushing things out and pulling things in that nature don't mean to line up like that, it's the same thing as lying to God and think he don't know no better."

I said, "You got that right."

"You ain't from around here, are you?"

"Not since I was real little. My daddy was a fisherman. I'm just passing through, wanted to stop here for old times' sake."

"Not many fishermen come here anymore. Mostly just a bunch of scum."

She arched a meaningful eyebrow at a man at a table behind us, and I swiveled in my chair to get a better look at him. Caucasian, wide shoulders, big hands. He could have been one of the men who helped Vern kidnap me, but then so could most of the other men in the downrun bar.

The waitress leaned down and lowered her voice. "If that creep bothers you, you let me know."

Somebody hollered for a refill, and she swished away with her back muscles rippling so the mermaid tattoo undulated.

The creep she'd singled out had an empty pitcher of beer on his table and a half-filled mug. From his flush-faced, loose-lipped scowl, he looked as if he'd already emptied several pitchers.

Cupcake straightened in his seat and yelled loud enough for everybody in the bar to hear. "Hey, sweetheart, my buddy over here's running low. Bring him a fresh pitcher!"

The waitress whirled and stared at Cupcake, then looked at me as if I'd betrayed her. I shrugged and rolled my eyes, a woman-to-woman message that said I wasn't to be held responsible for the dumb things any man did. She did the same eye-roll, and in a minute plopped down a full pitcher of beer at the next table. The man looked up at her stupidly, too drunk to realize what was going on.

In a nanosecond, Cupcake had scooted his chair across the grimy floor to the man's table. "Drink's on me, buddy! We gotta stick together."

A little bit of drool moistened the corners of the man's lips when he grinned. "Schtick together!"

Cupcake said, "Yes sir, me and my other buddy here have been where you are. We know what it's like to be out of work, no paycheck. Man, it's rough! Now we're in the money, we help out our buddies."

The man squinted and frowned. "I ain't out of work. Got a good job."

Zack stood up, dragged his chair to the man's table, and sat down as delicately as a Sunday school teacher. "It's okay, friend. Nothing to be ashamed about. Lots of good men out of work right now."

Red-faced, the man sat as upright as he could manage. "Nah, nah, I'm telling you, man, I got a good job. Big job. Hell, my boss owns this place!"

Zack said, "This bar?"

"No, man! This whole place! All of it!"

His voice heavy with sarcasm, Cupcake said, "You saying you work for Jeb Bush or somebody like that?"

"I'm saying Jeb Bush probably works for my boss."

Cupcake drawled, "But you can't tell us your boss's name, right? We just have to take your word for it."

"Kantor Tucker! That's who I work for! You know who that is? He's big, man. Got a plane bigger than the President's, more money than God. He says jump, everybody else says, 'How high?'"

Zack and Cupcake exchanged the kind of grins adults show when a small child tells a big bragging lie.

Cupcake said, "Friend, I was born in the morning, but not *this* morning. I don't believe you work for Kantor Tucker. If you did, you'd be swilling beer at the Ritz, not emptying pitchers in this dump."

The man blinked as if Cupcake had made a good point in a debate. "I never said I worked *directly* for Kantor Tucker. Not *directly* directly. I work for the man that's Tuck's right-hand man. That's what his friends call him, Tuck."

Zack sloshed beer into the man's mug. "So you work for a bigshot who works for Tucker. We apologize for thinking you weren't important. It must be something to work for a man smart enough to be Kantor Tucker's right-hand man."

The man managed a sneering grin while he took a long pull from his mug, but not without letting beer run down his chin. "He ain't all that smart. And he won't be a bigshot long. To tell the truth, Vern's too dumb to breathe on his own. If I didn't point him in the right direction, he'd screw up everything he does. Like the other day we were sup-posed to pick up a woman and take her to Tuck. You know what Vern did? He got the wrong woman! Can you beat that? The wrong damn woman! Tuck was some steamed."

I froze in my chair for a second, then relaxed. The guy was so drunk he wouldn't have recognized me if I'd ripped off my cap and glasses and danced on his table.

Carefully, Zack said, "I guess old Vern shaped up after pulling that stunt."

"Nah, he didn't change a bit. Dumb shit got his ass in a wringer for sure today."

Cupcake pulled his lips back in a fake smile. "What'd he do, grab another wrong woman?"

The drunk leaned forward in a conspiratorial hunch. "See, Tuck sent us to get a kid for a friend of his. I don't know the whole story but I think the friend was tired of paying child support to his ex-wife so Tuck was helping him out."

For a second, the inanity of what he was saying seemed to seep into some of his brain cells, and his head lifted a fraction as if he might be about to think.

Zack intercepted the urge with a laugh. "Man, I wish I could have somebody take my kid away from my ex-wife so I wouldn't have to pay the gold-digging bitch any more money."

The drunk's chest swelled with pride. "Well, Vern couldn't have done it without me. See, Vern has this big-ass limo he uses to drive celebrities and people like that around, so he parked it behind a vacant house next door to where the kid's mother lived. He sneaked in the side door of the woman's house and planted some nitrous oxide to make it look like this race car driver did it. Somebody Tuck has a grudge against, I guess. Anyway, while Vern grabbed the kid and set off a big fire in the room, I went down an alley to another house and got this Mexican woman Tuck had hired to take care of the kid. I led her to the limo, Vern came with the kid, and we took off."

Cupcake said, "Sounds like it went off okay. Where's the screw-up in that?"

The drunk looked as if he might cry at the enormity of Vern's mistake. "We were supposed to leave them in a house, the woman and the kid, but when we got there Vern got horny and put some moves on the woman and she ran away. Just ran out the front door and disappeared in the woods." He slumped in his chair, shaking his head at the memory.

My hands were clenched into such hard fists that my knuckles were frozen in place.

Cupcake poured more beer into the man's mug. "She take the kid with her?"

"Nah, she left it with us. Vern was all for us leaving it there in the house, but when I told him the woman was probably calling Tuck right then, he got scared. He was already in deep shit with Tuck, and Tuck ain't the kind of man to mess around with. So Vern left the kid with me and took off in the limo to look for the woman."

Cupcake said, "So you and the kid were alone in the house?"

"See, that's what I was thinking. I'm in the house with a kid we stole, and Vern's out driving up and down country roads, and the Mexican woman's out there somewhere, and what if cops come looking for the kid? They're going to think I'm the one that took it, and they ain't gonna believe all I did was walk a babysitter to a car, you know? So I got the hell out of there. Walked down Gator Trail to the highway to Arcadia, got a bus to Bradenton, got a cab to bring me here. I don't want to be anywhere around when they find that kid."

I felt a thrill of optimism. We practically had an address!

At some unspoken accord, Zack and Cupcake stood. With Cupcake frowning and towering over him, Zack looked like a skinny kid standing up to the town bully. They tossed a handful of bills on the drunk's table, and then some on mine.

Cupcake said, "Good luck, old buddy."

The drunk grinned at them in sloppy gratitude. They had made him feel important. For a few minutes he had forgotten that he was one of the world's losers, a piece of slag at the bottom of society's barrel. He had enough beer in him to turn his brain to mush and enough ego-stroking from Cupcake and Zack to make him completely ignore the fact that they'd left me alone while they talked to him.

I waved goodbye to the waitress and we got out as fast as possible. Outside, we grinned at one another like happy hounds.

I said, "Arcadia is forty miles from here."

Cupcake said, "Highway Seventy-two goes to Arcadia. Right through the alligator swamps."

Zack said, "We can look for Gator Trail on the map."

If any of us considered that Gator Trail might run for miles and have a hundred houses on it, we ignored the thought. Neither did we let ourselves think of the probable tangle of back sand roads, falling-in houses, and rusty squatter campers around Arcadia. Or the bleak image of a four-month-old baby left alone in an empty house. Or, if Vern had returned, under the care of a man known to be both a kidnapper and attempted rapist.

If we had let ourselves think of those things, hopelessness would have swallowed us entirely. Every minute that passed lessened the probability of finding Opal, and we were elated to have *any* landmark to go by.

Zack said, "Shouldn't go in daylight where they'd see us."

I said, "We'll have to be very discreet. And very careful."

Cupcake said, "She means don't tell your old man what we're doing."

Zack grimaced. "Don't worry."

I said, "What time?"

They both looked at their watches—big silver things with lots of little dials on their faces that probably told the time in every capital of the world, along with the humidity and temperature.

Zack said, "The sun sets early now."

It was true, and my inner coward shivered at the thought of driving through alligators in the dark. It's scary enough to be close to alligators when the sun's shining on them. I sure as heck didn't want to be with them at night.

Zack and Cupcake exchanged a look. Zack said, "We have some things to line up. Phone calls to make, things like that, and it may take some time."

"Phone calls?"

"Nothing about this. It's okay."

I didn't believe him. I thought he was planning something he didn't want me to know about, and that Cupcake knew what it was and approved. But if I said anything more, he might cut me out of the trip altogether. He was, after all, Opal's father and Ruby's husband. I was merely a pet sitter with a personal attachment to his wife and baby.

Zack said, "We'll leave no later than eight." For a skinny kid, he was surprisingly decisive.

We agreed that I would meet them at Zack's place, and we all got into our vehicles and went off to our respective responsibilities.

Personally, I drove off with my blood singing. I was taking action to find Opal. Her father was taking action. A strong athlete was taking action. We weren't passive, we weren't letting Myra Kreigle and Kantor Tucker get away with kidnapping Opal.

I was halfway to Tom Hale's condo for my first afternoon pet visit before I remembered that Guidry planned to make dinner for me that night.

That's another glitch in having a man in your life. As soon as you're a couple instead of a single, you have to coordinate schedules, arrange meeting times and places, get your life organized around an *us* instead of a *me*. Sometimes that's comfortable and nice. Sometimes it's a royal pain in the kazoo. I loved having Guidry in my life, but little pieces of myself seemed to have floated off when I wasn't looking. I needed to pull them back in.

# 24

Morning or afternoon, I usually spend a good half hour at each pet's house, so that seven or eight pet calls take at least four hours. Add to that travel time and the extra time some calls need because a dog needs extra cheering up or a cat requires some premium cuddling, and it can take five hours. But that afternoon I cut all the visits short.

Tom Hale was working at his kitchen table when I arrived at his condo, and only waved hello. I was glad, because I didn't want to take any chances of slipping up and telling him what I was going to do when I finished afternoon rounds. Billy Elliot had to be content with only one lap around the parking lot. He seemed a little puzzled, but wagged his tail in forgiveness when I told him I had to go look for a missing baby. That's the neat thing about pets. You can trust them to keep your secrets.

All the other clients were cats. Every cat got petted and given fresh food and water. Every litter box got cleaned. But that was it. No cuddling, no games of chase-the-ball or leap-for-the-peacock-feather. It was strictly a no-frills afternoon. I explained the reason to each cat, and I solemnly promised that I would make it up to them on the next visit. Each one listened to me with the royally benign tolerance that only a cat can bestow on a human.

After the last pet visit, I swung by Mr. Stern's house, where a van was parked at the curb. It looked innocuous, but I was sure it was manned by an officer monitoring phone calls. If no ransom demand was made within the first twenty-four hours of Opal's kidnapping, the sheriff's department would call in the FBI. I was sure nobody would call to ask for money. Opal's kidnappers didn't want money, they wanted silence.

I still considered myself on the job for Cheddar, so I called the Victim's Assistance Unit of the sheriff's department for the name of the hotel where they'd taken Mr. Stern and Ruby. Whenever a crime or fire leaves a family homeless, Victim's Assistance puts them up in a hotel, gives them emotional support, and makes arrangements for whatever they need. At the hotel, the desk clerk rang their suite and got permission for me to go up to see them.

Ruby opened the door to the suite and stepped aside to let me in. Behind her, voices murmured on a TV.

She said, "Granddad's gone back to the animal hospital to be with Cheddar."

"Is he okay?"

"Granddad or Cheddar?"

"Both."

"The vet says Cheddar could go home tonight if he had a home to go to. Granddad's sad and worried."

On the TV, the volume rose for breaking news. "Zack

Carlyle's kidnapped baby still hasn't been found. Police have issued an appeal to people in Florida and Alabama to be on the lookout for a woman named Doreen Antone. She is believed to be traveling north toward Alabama. Her sister in Alabama says she has not heard from her and does not believe she would kidnap a baby. Antone's parents also say kidnapping is not something their daughter would do."

A quick clip of a harried-looking older couple flashed on the screen, with the woman saying, "We raised our daughters right. Doreen wouldn't do nothing like that."

They were replaced by a photograph of Opal, and then a grainy snapshot of the cleaning woman when she was much younger and slimmer.

The announcer pressed on. "Antone's former boy-friend, Billy Clyde Ray, has told investigators that Antone had been depressed since giving birth to a stillborn infant six weeks ago. Ray says he has not seen Antone for over a month and does not know anything about the baby's kidnapping. He is considered a person of interest in the case, but the sheriff's office stressed that Ray is not a suspect, merely one who might have important information."

Ruby stared woodenly at the set. If she was offended that Opal was identified as "Zack Carlyle's baby," she didn't show it. I whirled to the TV set and turned it off.

"Ruby, are you sure you're doing the right thing?"

For a second, she seemed to consider pretending not to know what I meant, then dropped it.

"I was a fool to think I could go up against Myra and Tuck."

"But you can't let them—"

"I have to. I'll have a terrible case of amnesia at Myra's trial. I won't be able to remember a single detail of what I saw while I worked for her. I won't remember anything about Tuck being involved in her business. I won't remember a name or a date or an offshore account. I won't remember a thing."

"And then?"

"Then I'll go to prison and Opal will live. She'll even live well. While I'm in prison, she'll have a nice home with a kind person to take care of her. She'll be well fed and healthy."

I had to make an effort to make my mouth work. "How can you be sure of that?"

"I know Myra. She's a piranha when it comes to money or business deals, but she was like a mother to me when I needed one, and it wasn't an act. She'll make sure Opal gets good care."

I couldn't think of a thing to say. As much as it broke her heart, Ruby had analyzed the situation with cold logic, and she'd made the only decision that would save her baby's life. And I knew she had the terrible and wondrous strength to follow through with it.

I said, "Ruby, the other woman I saw in Myra's house looked like a kind, caring woman."

She licked dry lips. "You think she's the one they got to take care of Opal?"

"I think it's possible."

The hope in her eyes was pitiful. "And she seemed kind?"

"She did."

Stumbling backward, she sank to the edge of the hotel bed.

Even though I knew it might not be true, I wanted to tell her that her husband and I were going with Cupcake to rescue Opal. Instead, I said, "You're a strong woman, Ruby. You'll get through this."

Ruby closed her eyes and rolled onto the bed with her back to me. I touched her ankle lightly and left her. There was nothing else for either of us to say.

The sun was about three hours higher in the sky than usual when I got home. Paco's truck was in the carport and Ella wasn't in my apartment. Michael wouldn't be home until the next morning.

As soon as I was inside my apartment, I called Guidry.

"Could we do supper early? I'm really beat, and I need to go to bed early."

He didn't exactly jump at the idea, but he agreed. I told him I'd be at his place in an hour, and stepped into a hard-driving warm shower. I let the spray unsnarl some of the kinks in my muscles. I shampooed my hair and shaved my legs. I used a buffing thing on my heels and elbows to make my skin silky smooth. That's another thing about having a man in your life. You make sure nothing will snag on any of your corners. Besides, I might get killed that night, and I didn't want to leave life with stubble on my legs.

With a quick slide of lip gloss and a touch of blush, I hurried to my closet-office, pushed stuff around, and chose a short khaki skirt and a crisp white shirt. With a cool raffia belt and the shirt sleeves rolled partway up, I looked casual but a little dressed up. I added a string of pearls to

peep from under the shirt, a couple of slim silver brace-
lets, and stepped into linen espadrilles with tall heels. If I
say so myself, I looked damn good.

I'd never been to his house before, but I knew Guidry
lived in a small stucco bungalow a stone's throw from Siesta Key's business district. The yard had the look of being
cared for by efficient professionals who trimmed with
more haste than love. A small front porch needed sweeping, and a spiderweb stretched across the front door in a
sure giveaway that Guidry entered and exited the house
through a door in the attached garage.

I rang the bell. Guidry opened the door with the web
hanging between us like an unreliable lifeline. He swat-
ted it away, and I stepped inside.

The house had the same easy elegance Guidry has: polished concrete floors the color of old copper, a wall of
books, black leather furniture, Mission-style tables, big
plush pillows in rough textured fabric, standing swing-
arm architect lamps, and a sound system playing soft jazz.
No window coverings except wooden louvered shutters.
Pure Guidry.

The only surprise was that Guidry wore jeans and a
T-shirt. The jeans were plain worn Levi's and the T-shirt
was ordinary white cotton. Seeing him in faded jeans
was like seeing him naked, only I'd already seen him naked and he'd looked as elegant without clothes as he did
in designer linen. Jeans were something else. Jeans erased
an invisible line that had been drawn between us. Jeans
said he was on my team.

We stood and looked at each other for a long moment,
then came together like two magnets drawn by forces

preordained. Have I mentioned that Guidry is a great kisser?

Oh, yes, he is.

When we finally came up for air, he rubbed his thumb across my jawline and smiled down at me. I'm always shocked at those moments of seeing him vulnerable. Shocked and a little scared. I don't want another person's happiness in my hands. It's too much responsibility. I might fail.

I said, "What brought on this urge to cook?"

"I know how much you like to eat, so I thought I'd better start feeding you. Besides, I want to talk to you about something."

There it was again, that something he wanted to talk to me about. I caught a glint of apprehension in his eyes that scared me. Whatever he wanted to talk to me about was something he dreaded.

"Is it about Opal?"

"Who?"

"The baby that was kidnapped."

"No, nothing like that."

"Then what?"

"Later. First we have to cook."

*We?*

I followed him into a kitchen that was bigger than mine, but looked the same—a room where not much cooking got done. On the countertop, he had assembled a stack of lasagna noodles, some cheese, some cans of tomatoes and sauce, and several jars of seasonings. My brother would have looked at that collection and felt the thrill of challenge, a zippy bubble in the blood that comes from delight. I looked at it and saw tomato spatters, pasta paste, cheese gunk, a huge mess to clean up.

For a few seconds, we stood staring at all the ingredients, suddenly awkward as two people who'd somehow landed on the moon at the same time.

Guidry said, "I've never asked, but do you cook?"

"Of course I cook."

"What?"

"Are you going deaf?"

"I meant what do you cook."

I felt a little panicky. I boil eggs. I scramble eggs. I heat soup. I make salads, both green and tuna. I can even make pancakes from scratch. But with a brother who's not only a great cook but loves to feed everybody he knows, I've never been *called* to cook much.

I said, "What were you planning?"

He looked as if he'd caught my panic. "Ah, I got this stuff for lasagna. You like lasagna?"

"Sure."

"My mother makes it with sweet Italian sausage and ground turkey, so I got some. Also some ricotta cheese, parmesan cheese, and mozzarella cheese."

He waved a hand at the assemblage on the counter. "I got lots of stuff."

I had a sudden image of him calling his mother in New Orleans and asking her how to make lasagna. I doubted he had ever made it in his life. I doubted he had ever even *watched* anybody make it. That made two of us.

I took a deep, measured breath. I smiled. "You have wine?"

"Good Chianti."

"Okay then. Let's do this."

I felt a surge of confidence. We were going to be okay, Guidry and I. We were going to make dinner together. We were going to work smoothly together the way happily married couples do. We were going to join our talents and our energies and produce something wonderful.

It's a wonder bluebirds didn't pick up the dish towels and fly around the kitchen with them. Or that rose petals didn't drift from the ceiling and settle on my shoulders. I was that goofy.

# 25

Twenty minutes later, the sweet Italian sausage was sizzling in a big pot on the stove and Guidry no longer looked like a way fine homicide detective. He looked like a man with a shiny forehead and a T-shirt with a meat-juice stain across the chest. Personally, I was chopping onions at the narrow counter beside the sink while holding a bleeding finger well away from the knife blade. I had wrapped a paper towel around my nicked fingertip to soak up the blood, but it was still a little oozy. I suspected I'd smeared blood on my face when I wiped away onion-chopping tears. And all the time I chopped and wept, my mind kept going to Opal, with quick awful glimpses of terrible things that could be happening to her.

Guidry was equally subdued. No easy banter like the kind in Michael's kitchen while he cooked. We worked like convicts in a prison kitchen.

While the sausage fried, Guidry consulted scrawled directions—I'd been right, he'd called his mother—and then brought all the jars of spices to the counter where I worked.

He said, "I was supposed to get fresh basil, and I got dried."

With my eyes streaming tears from the onions, I looked up at him and forced my hand not to wipe at my face. "I think dried would be okay."

"Yeah, but how much? What's the dried equivalent of a half cup of chopped basil?"

It was downright pathetic that he thought I'd know that.

A burning odor caught our attention, and we turned to see billows of dark smoke rising from the big pan where the sausage fried. Guidry swore and ran to jerk the pan from the heat while I ran around opening cupboard doors. I think I left some blood smears on some of them.

He said, "What are you doing?"

"Looking for a fire extinguisher."

"It's not a fire, it's just smoke."

I wrapped a clean paper towel around my bleeding fingertip and came and stood beside him. We looked at blackened links of sausage in the skillet. The oil they'd been burning in was black too.

I said, "I think you're supposed to take the casings off the sausage before you fry it."

"You sure?"

"That's what Michael does. Then while it fries he sort of mashes it around to break it up."

"Well, we can't use this burned stuff. Do you suppose the sausage part is vital?"

We looked at the package of uncooked ground turkey

waiting on the countertop. At the rate we were going, it would be midnight before we got all those layers of noodles and cheese and meat stacked in a pan. It might be even later before we managed to make a decent sauce. I had appointments I couldn't do later. I pushed my folded shirtsleeves higher on my arms. Somehow both sleeves had acquired black marks. Also some mystery stains that might or might not be my own blood.

I said, "I don't think cooking lasagna is our thing."

Guidry had burned a finger. The burn looked as if it would soon blister. He blew on it and looked glum.

He said, "Let's do what we should have done in the first place. You call the pizza place while I clean up this mess. We'll talk in the living room."

I gave him a grateful smile, but behind my smile I was scared. He wanted to talk about something important, and I was afraid of what he wanted to say. He'd said it wasn't about Opal, but I couldn't think of anything else that would make his eyes get that wary look, like he didn't want to tell me something that had to be told.

While Guidry made clean-up noises in the kitchen, I phoned for pizza, antipasti, and cannoli in the living room. I found Guidry's bathroom, which was almost tragically clean and neat. Recessed lighting, round marble sinks with shiny chrome faucets arched so tall you could wash a dog under them. Not that Guidry ever would. Thick brown towels so plush that after I splashed water on my face and washed away onion and smoke damage, I patted myself dry with a tissue from a sleek brown box on the counter.

I resisted an impulse to slide open wide mirrored

doors on a medicine cabinet and look for Band-Aids. Just because we were a couple didn't give me the right to snoop. Well, it sort of did, but my finger had pretty much stopped bleeding, and I didn't want Guidry to think I'd been in his medicine cabinet. I made a neat wrapper out of toilet paper and went back to the living room.

Two glasses of red wine sat on the big square coffee table. Candles were lit and the lamps were turned low. Soft jazz cooed from hidden speakers. I took a deep breath, slipped out of my shoes, and settled into the corner of one of the matching sofas.

Guidry brought a stack of plates to put on the coffee table, along with enough paper napkins to blot up the BP Gulf oil spill. He had cleaned up too, dried the sheen on his forehead, changed into a fresh T-shirt. He took a chair kitty-cornered from me, toed off his leather sandals, and put his feet on the coffee table. He had elegant feet. Long and slim, with smooth toenails. I wondered if he got pedicures.

I lifted my own pink-nailed feet onto the coffee table and raised my glass of wine to make a toast.

He said, "What happened to your finger?"

"I just nipped it a little bit while I was chopping onions."

"You want a Band-Aid?"

"No, it's fine."

I held my glass up again. "Here's to ordering pizza!"

He grinned and raised his own glass. "Amen!"

We sipped wine, we smiled at each other, we waited for the doorbell to ring with the pizza. And whatever Guidry wanted to tell me slinked around us with a sly grin on its sneaky face.

The pizza delivery came while we were still on our first glasses of wine. Guidry padded barefoot to the door, paid the guy, and came back balancing some big bags atop a huge flat pizza box.

He said, "What'd you do, order one of everything?"

I shrugged. "I worked up an appetite chopping those onions."

He spread it all out on the coffee table and for a few minutes we were too busy organizing stuff on our plates to talk. Then for a few more minutes we were too busy chewing and swallowing. In spite of myself, my scatty mind went to Ruby and Mr. Stern, caromed to Opal, then looped to Zack and his uptight father. While I'd watched Ruby and Zack together that afternoon, it had been obvious they loved each other. Zack was wrong not to trust Ruby, and Ruby had been wrong to take Opal and leave him.

I said, "Ruby and Zack are both good people. They're just young. They don't know yet how precious every moment is. If they had played their lives differently, they could have made a good home for Opal."

Guidry put his slice of pizza on his plate and leaned forward to set it on the coffee table. He took a sip of wine and studied my face.

He said, "You'd like to have another baby, wouldn't you?"

I was so shocked that I had to remove my feet from the coffee table and sit up straight to stare at him. "Why do you think that?"

"Well, for one thing, we weren't talking about the Carlyles. And for another, when you talk about babies, you get a look."

"I do not."

His eyes were sad. "No kidding, Dixie, would you like to have another baby? We've never talked about it, and we should."

I suddenly felt the same way I'd felt several weeks before—when I'd jumped into the bay to save a woman and been under water longer than I could hold my breath. In that watery blackness, I had felt blind, clawing panic, and that's what I felt now. I had only recently got over irrational guilt for replacing my dead husband. I certainly wasn't prepared to talk about replacing my dead child.

I slammed my plate on the coffee table and stomped to the bathroom, where I stood panting in front of the mirror over the sink. Staring at my flushed face and blazing eyes, I had one of those out-of-context memories that carry important messages. This one was about the first crack I had seen in my parents' marriage. I had been about five, and I remembered watching my mother dress for a Bruce Springsteen concert in Tampa. She had worn a skirt so short her legs seemed to go on forever, and she and my dad had argued about it. He thought it was too revealing and she thought he was a prude. They were still arguing when they came home hours later, and from my bed I'd heard my dad say he'd lost all respect for my mother when she took off her panties and offered them to Springsteen. The Boss hadn't taken them, and my dad said that showed how inappropriate she'd been.

The memory had surfaced off and on all my life, the way childhood memories of quarreling parents will, but now for the first time I saw it from an adult woman's perspective. Viewed that way, I imagined my mother had felt so humiliated at being rejected by Springsteen that she couldn't forgive my father for witnessing it. Somehow that insight helped me calm down and look at my own situation from an adult's perspective.

I didn't feel humiliated by Guidry's question. I even recognized that it was a reasonable question for a man to ask. But it had stirred up emotions and memories that I wasn't yet ready to visit, and I wished he hadn't asked it. Guidry had no children, and now I wondered if that was because of circumstance or design. I wished I didn't wonder that, because it might change something between us if I found out he didn't want children. I truly hadn't considered having another baby, but some day I *might*, and I wished he hadn't forced me to consider it.

I slid open a mirrored door on his medicine cabinet and found a box of Band-Aids. His razor was on a shelf, and some shaving cream. I didn't look at anything else. I put a Band-Aid on my finger, replaced the box, and stood a few more minutes to be sure I could talk without weeping or losing my cool.

I must have stayed in the bathroom a long time, because when I went back to the living room, Guidry was asleep on the sofa. He felt me beside him and opened his eyes. He held out his hand and I sat down next to him.

He said, "I was insensitive. I'm sorry."

When a man already knows what he's done wrong, there's not much to say.

"I'm just not ready for it yet."

"That's what made it insensitive. I'm sorry."

Maybe it was because I didn't want to talk about babies as a possibility for myself. Or maybe it was because I just wanted to deflect attention from myself. Whatever, I wasn't able to talk about babies in general without talking about Opal in particular. I decided I couldn't keep the secret about Myra and Tucker being behind Opal's kidnapping away from Guidry.

I said, "If we're going to have an honest relationship, we have to share what's going on in our lives."

Guidry looked contrite. "Dixie, I've been offered a job with the New Orleans Police Department."

"*What?*"

"I'm sorry I haven't told you. It just never seemed like the right time."

I heard a tinny ringing in my ears. "What are you going to do?"

"It's a good offer. I'd head up the homicide division. I'd be a part of rebuilding my city."

The buzzing in my ears got louder, with replays of every conversation Guidry and I had ever had about New Orleans. His family lived there, he'd grown up there, his roots were there. It was his passionate love for the city that had pushed me over the edge into falling in love with him.

I sat on his black leather sofa and looked at all the Italian food on the coffee table. I was sorry I'd ordered so much. Sorry I'd mentioned Opal. Sorry the evening was ending dark and bent as a stubbed-out cigarette.

I said, "You've already decided to take it, haven't you?"

"I wanted to talk to you first."

It was a lie. He may have *wanted* to talk to me before he made the decision, but the decision had probably been made at the moment the offer was proffered. New Orleans was as much a part of Guidry as Siesta Key was a part of me.

We stared into each other's eyes with all our unspoken fears and hopes exposed like naked corpses.

Guidry said, "The city is struggling to recapture its soul. A lot of its heart and talent and love and laughter left with the people who were driven out of flooded homes. Artists and musicians and cooks, generations of families. They want to come back, but a lot of them don't have anything to come back *to*. I want to help rebuild. Not just neighborhoods, but the police department too. New Orleans law enforcement officers tolerated corruption too long. But when the levees broke, crooked cops ran like rats. Now that the department is free of them, they're starting over with a clean slate."

His voice slowed to a trickle. "I guess what it comes down to is that my awareness of belonging to something larger than myself is rooted in memories of growing up in New Orleans. Those memories call to me."

I completely understood because the same memories of Sarasota called to me.

Woodenly, I slipped my shoes on and stood up. "I have to go home. I can't talk now."

He rose too, and touched my arm. "We could make it work, Dixie."

He meant marriage, living together in New Orleans, making a life together there.

I said, "I can't think now."

He leaned down and kissed my forehead. Tenderly, the way people kiss a dead person at a memorial service.

"I love you, Dixie."

I touched my open palm to the side of his face. "I know you do."

# 26

I drove home on autopilot, feeling light-headed and weird, caught between a future that could be completely different than the one I'd always imagined, and a past that would always be a part of who I was.

I was shocked at the idea of Guidry moving away, shocked at how I'd reacted when he'd told me. When Todd and I were together, I would have followed him to another continent. Why was I so disturbed at the idea of moving to New Orleans with Guidry?

I didn't think it was because I loved Guidry less. It was more that I loved me more. I'd worked too hard at learning to be at home in the person I was to abandon that person. And I wasn't sure I'd still be me if I moved away from the Key, where I was a part of every grain of sand on the beaches. I had to decide how far love can stretch, how much it can remold you and reshape you and leave you glad you've changed.

If I went to New Orleans, I'd be somebody else, and there was no guarantee I'd be comfortable as somebody else. If I ended up hating the person I became after I went with Guidry to New Orleans, I'd no longer love him either. And I knew, with a terrible awareness, that Guidry feared the same thing was happening to him, that he was losing himself away from his beloved New Orleans. If he did, he would lose his love for me.

There was another factor that I'd never considered until this evening, but now I had to look at it. When my little girl died, a part of me had died with her. I'd never expected to have another baby. I hadn't wanted another baby. But now that Guidry had forced the issue, I felt the idea nibbling at the edges of my mind, and I wasn't sure I wanted to push it away.

Guidry had been right when he said we'd never discussed the possibility of us having babies together. Now it seemed strange that we hadn't. Even stranger was that I had no idea why Guidry and his ex-wife hadn't had children. I should have known something that important. I should have asked if their childlessness had been by choice. More specifically, whose choice? If Guidry didn't want children, I should know that. Not that I wanted to have a baby, but someday I *might*.

I thought about Ruby and Zack, and how their love had become diseased by bitterness and distrust. Had they chosen to have Opal, or had she come as a fortunate accident? If Ruby went to prison and Opal was spirited away to live someplace with Angelina, Ruby and Zack would never have a second chance to create a family. They would suffer the loss, but Opal would suffer more.

In an ideal world—one in which I made all the rules—everybody's drinking water would contain birth control chemicals. Consenting adults could screw around all they wanted to. They could fall in love, out of love, break people's hearts and have their own hearts broken. They could spend all their money, gamble it away, or stuff it down a rat hole. They could live as selfishly as they wanted for as long as they wanted.

But if a couple decided to have children, they would have to pass rigorous tests of character and kindness and good humor. They would have to prove they were responsible people with the ability to provide a good home, medical care, and education for a child. They would also have to agree to stay together for the rest of their lives, and swear that if something went wrong in their relationship they'd damn well fix it. Only then would I issue the antidote to the birth control chemicals.

Turning down the drive to my apartment jerked me back to reality. I didn't run the world, I wasn't married or pregnant and might never be again, and any decision I made about moving with Guidry to New Orleans would have to be made later.

At home, I was glad that Paco was inside the house with Ella. If I hurried, I might be able to leave for the trip to Arcadia without lying about where I was going. Upstairs in my apartment, I hurried to change clothes. I kept the lace underwear on. If I got killed trying to rescue Opal, at least I'd look good when people viewed my body. But when it came to outerwear, I chose tough. Faded jeans, a hooded black T, and a pair of sturdy boots.

I chose tough for accessories too. I got them from the secret drawer built into my bed's wooden frame. The drawer was custom designed to hold my guns—some that had once belonged to Todd and some that had been my own off-duty guns. Always cleaned, oiled, and ready for use, they lie in special niches inside the drawer. I'm qualified on all of them, but my favorite is a sweet five-shot J-frame .38. With its black rubber grip, stainless steel barrel and cylinder, it's lightweight and easy to slip into a pocket. No safety levers to think about, no magazines to fail. It was the perfect weapon for the night's mission.

I picked the revolver out of its niche, slid it into the back of my jeans, and pushed a couple of filled speed loaders into my pockets. Then, fully armed with lipstick, lace underwear, and revolver, I headed out to meet Zack and Cupcake.

Every civilized person knows that violence of any kind is the ultimate admission of failure. Whether it's between individuals or between nations, it points to a level of ignorance or stupidity or laziness too profound to resolve grievances with words or compromise. But if I had to shoot somebody in order to save Opal, I wouldn't hesitate for a nanosecond.

Zack's property—his home and adjacent race shop—was on the southeast side of Sarasota county, one of the few spreads still immune to developers and gated communities. A flush of twilight still lingered on the western horizon when I arrived at a gate blocking the entrance to Zack's tree-thick property. The gate was wrought iron, with a design of a race car worked into the bars. Through the gate, I could see a neat frame house set under oaks and pines, with a green lawn that looked as if somebody gave it careful attention.

A double-decker transport van sat beyond the house on an immaculate paved area in front of a long, low building with an open front. The building looked somewhat like an automotive repair shop, with tools and auto parts hanging on the back wall, a row of new tires along the side, and a pit in the center with a rack for lifting a car overhead. There were also several things I didn't recognize, like a couple of metal frames that looked as if they'd been designed to fit inside a gutted car. A black Chevy Camaro with rusty spots on its fenders was angled on the pavement in front of the garage's open bay doors. Several other vintage cars were parked to the side.

I rolled to the ubiquitous security station, pressed a button, and waited for a human voice to ask my business. In this case, the human voice was gruff and male.

I said, "I'm Dixie Hemingway."

The voice became gruffer. "Wait for the gate to open."

The gate parted, and I rolled into a parking lot that quickly filled with a throng of men.

Zack came to my window. "Some of my friends have come to help."

One by one, men with grim faces stepped forward to shake my hand through the car window. They looked at me hard in the eyes, as if they were taking my measure.

Cupcake stood to the side watching them.

With all that testosterone, an argument was bound to start. Zack and Cupcake immediately got into a debate over which car we should use, while the other guys offered grunts of agreement or dissent.

Zack wanted to drive one of his race cars because it was faster. Half the other men thought that was a good idea. But Cupcake argued that he and I should ride in the same car with Zack, and Zack's car only held one person. I didn't understand why it only held one person, but if that was its limit, Cupcake was obviously right.

Raising my voice over the male ones, I said, "My Bronco sits high and has plenty of room."

A dozen heads tilted down to look at me, a dozen pairs of eyes registered surprised respect that I had an opinion.

Zack said, "No speed."

Cupcake said, "Don't need speed, bro."

With a broad dimpled grin at me, he lumbered to the Bronco, wriggled his bulk into the backseat, and leaned back like a maharaja waiting for his elephant to carry him where he wanted to go.

Zack turned to the other men. "Okay, stay connected. I'll keep you informed. When it's time, we'll put the plan into action. You know what to do."

I didn't know what their plan was, but there were immediate nods, back-slapping, and words of agreement. The men walked off to cars parked beside Zack's home race shop. Those cars didn't look like they'd make it to the end of the block. But men got inside them—one man to a car—started growling engines, and sat waiting for Zack to lead the way.

I saw Zack's father looking out the front window of the house. He did not look happy.

As Zack got into the front passenger seat of the Bronco and belted up, I noticed that he wore a wireless phone clip on his right ear.

I said, "Would one of you like to tell me what's going on?"

Zack did a rolling motion with his hand. "We'll fill you in on the way."

I didn't have an option. I could go under Zack's terms or not at all. When I turned the ignition key, Zack watched my hand as if he doubted I had sense enough to drive. I goosed the Bronco a little bit to give it a macho sound, and we sailed through Zack's gate.

On Clark Road out of Sarasota, I looked at Zack's profile and wondered what was going through his mind. Athletes have always been a mystery to me, and drag racers were an even bigger mystery. I was beginning to realize that drag racers have to be more calculating and deliberate than other athletes. They're more in competition with themselves than with other racers, and speed is only one component of the competition. The rest is about timing and fuel and precision, things that take intense focus.

I looked over my shoulder to see if the other cars were close behind us, but Cupcake took up so much space that I couldn't see out the back window. He smiled at me when I looked back. He really did have the sweetest smile I'd ever seen.

Outside Sarasota, Clark Road becomes State Road 72, a stark two-lane highway edged by pines and oaks dripping gray moss like old men's beards. The highway runs due east to Arcadia, the only incorporated community in DeSoto County. Arcadia is a town of survivors. On Thanksgiving Day in 1905, it was destroyed by a fire that started in a livery stable. A century later, on Friday, August 13, 2004, the city was almost destroyed again by Hurricane Charley. Arcadia still depends primarily on agriculture for its economy, but it has reinvented itself as a tourist attraction for antiques lovers. People drive from miles around on Sundays just to eat a good country breakfast at one of their restaurants and shop in their antiques stores.

Along the highway, bridges span boggy swamps where giant alligators stretch themselves as if posing for tourist photos. Fields of cabbage palms harbor rattlesnakes. Orange groves and fields of ragweed are neighbors to fenced pastures where heat-tolerant Senepol cattle raise their smooth polled heads to look at passing cars. Turkey vultures circle fresh carcasses of small deer or wild pigs struck by speeding trucks. An occasional mailbox atop a post marks a dirt lane twisting to an old Florida world that will soon be extinct.

I drove with both hands on the wheel, careful around frequent twists in the road, imagining how terrifying it would have been for Angelina to hitchhike along this gator-edged highway. Large alligators are awesome animals. They consume anything that comes close to them. Tourists who underestimate their speed or ferocity have been known to lose a family pet to them.

When we were halfway to Arcadia, Zack said, "I looked up Gator Trail on the Internet. It intersects State Road Seventy-two a few miles this side of Arcadia. Just before Horse Creek."

He sounded as if everybody in Florida knew where Horse Creek was. Maybe they did and I was the only one who didn't.

I said, "Uh-huh."

In my rearview mirror, I could see headlights from a line of cars snaking behind us.

We ate up a few more miles and Zack spoke again. "About two years ago, some coyotes crammed a bunch of illegals inside a refrigerator truck and smuggled them into Florida. They dumped them in a house somewhere outside Arcadia and left them. Men, women, and children. They were all half dead from dehydration. Some of them died."

Cupcake said, "People shouldn't be treated like that."

Zack said, "The thing is, Myra Kreigle owned that house. I remember it because Ruby and I had just started dating, and Myra's name caught my attention. The police talked to her, but she claimed she didn't know anything about any smuggling. The police believed her, but now I wonder if she was in on the whole thing."

I said, "Do you remember where the house was?"

"Some place outside town."

Arcadia is edged by makeshift communities of tin-roof shacks and old mobile homes on dirt roads. As if he realized the futility of looking for Opal in any of those places, Zack went silent and still.

I said, "You promised to tell me why your friends are going with us. And let me just say, for the record, that I think it's a bad idea. We'll attract too much attention."

From the backseat, Cupcake said, "Tell her, bro."

Zack seemed to try to collect his thoughts. I had the feeling that racing came a lot easier to him than speech.

He said, "They're just coming along in case we need them. You know, safety in numbers, that kind of thing."

I could almost feel Cupcake's eyes roll at the way Zack had evaded the question. Zack didn't want to share his plan with me, and that was that.

I said, "We're getting close to Arcadia. Watch for Gator Trail."

Almost immediately, Cupcake said, "There's Horse Creek!"

A neat white rectangle low to the ground announced that Horse Creek lay directly ahead. Before we got to it, another well-painted sign at a blacktopped road announced Gator Trail. It seemed as if the entire universe had entered into a conspiracy to help us find Opal. First we'd got information about where Vern had left Opal, now there were signs to direct us. How much better could it get?

I made a sharp turn onto Gator Trail, amazed at how fortunate we were. I was sure we had lucked out, big time.

Somewhere, a donkey probably laughed.

# 27

As I turned onto Gator Trail, Zack mumbled something into his headset, and instead of turning with us, the line of cars behind us went straight over Horse Creek. In the side mirror, I watched their taillights pull to the shoulder and park half hidden under the trees.

I refused to ask why they weren't following us to the house. I supposed Zack had given them instructions. I supposed he and his racer friends had arrived at some kind of plan that seemed logical to them. Something told me I might be happier not knowing that plan.

Faint light from a rind of moon carved shallow pools in Gator Trail's unlit, single-lane blacktop. Our headlights cut a tunnel between a dark tangle of scrub pines, oat grass, conifers, mossy oaks, and palmettos on each side of the road.

Cupcake gestured toward the black silhouettes. "Wild hogs live in there. They come out at night to forage. During the day they dig holes to sleep in." He sounded as if his skin crawled at the thought.

I didn't want to think about those feral hogs. As ferocious as alligators, wild hogs are not choosy about what kind of flesh they eat.

After a mile or two, the road made a sharp right, but my headlights caught something on the left that made me stop, back up, and turn the Bronco left.

A decades-old sign almost hidden by brambles and tall weeds announced the entrance to Empire Estates. A second sign warned: NO TRESPASSING! RESIDENTS AND GUESTS ONLY!

The sign had been formed by wooden blue letters nailed to a white board, but the blue paint had crazed like old china, and the letters hung at dipsy angles. Beyond the sign, our headlights picked up the gleam of a white sand road so encroached upon by trees and underbrush that it was narrow as a cart trail. Once the entrance to a luxury retirement community, the broken sign and silver road were all that was left of failed hopes.

Cupcake said, "Somebody's been stuck."

Ahead on the road, tires had eaten deeply into sand and left two long furrows. The humped ridges reminded me of the way loggerhead turtles throw up piles of sand while they dig their nests. But we were a long way from loggerhead nesting grounds, and a different kind of reptile had made those furrows. Most likely, he had done it in a black limo with tinted windows.

Zack said, "Heavy car, too much speed for sand."

Cupcake said, "Locals would know better."

"Yup."

An explosion of light and an impatient honking sound made us all jerk and look out the rear window at a tall pickup. The truck's engine thrummed with the impatient energy of a motor prepared to roll over anything in its path. Praying the truck wasn't driven by one of Tucker's goons, I leaned out my window to get a look at the driver. It was a woman, and she looked like she was on her last nerve.

In half a nanosecond, I was out of the Bronco and trotting to the pickup. The woman had her window rolled down and an elbow resting on the frame.

I said, "Gosh, I'm sorry! I didn't see you back here! The thing is, I'm not even sure I'm on the right road, and when I saw how somebody had got stuck in the sand, I was afraid to go on."

She didn't smile, but the hard look in her eyes softened. "Yeah, some fool got stuck there. Big old black limo with a numb-nuts driver."

I said, "Oh God, I'll bet that was my crazy old uncle's driver. That's who I'm looking for. He's my mother's brother, and she's worried about him."

She perked up at the thought of my crazy old uncle. "He lives around here?"

"Well, that's the thing. He lives in Tampa, but he owns a house around here somewhere—I think it's on this road, but I'm not sure. He's rich as all get out, has a big black limo and a driver, more money than good sense, to tell the truth. Anyway, he told my mother he was going to come stay in his house down here for a few days. He's probably all right, but I promised my mother I'd check on him."

The woman took her elbow off the window frame to get down to dissing my crazy uncle.

"Only one house it could be. You go about a mile and then turn at the first right. It's about a half mile down. Mailbox at the road, but the house is behind trees. Nobody lives there, but every now and then you'll see several cars there. I always figured something hinky was going on in there, gambling or women or something. But we don't stick our noses in other people's business out here, you know?"

I looked at the bleak landscape of tall weeds and overgrown trees. "Doesn't look like many people live out here."

"Only a few of us. Most are mobile homes or RVs. We all know each other, watch out for each other. But that house is one nobody knows about."

I could tell she couldn't wait to spread the news about my rich uncle and his eccentric ways.

I said, "You think I can drive through that sand and not get stuck?"

"You just got to be careful, is all. Don't hit it hard."

"Actually, I think I'll skip it. If his limo driver was here this morning, then my uncle's fine. I'll get out of your way now."

I sprinted back to the Bronco and pulled it back to the main road so the woman could drive through the Empire Estates entrance. She tooted her horn and waved at me as she drove past. At the rutted sand, she slowed to a crawl and eased her way through.

Zack said, "What?"

"She said a black limo got stuck in the sand. Also said there's only one house where nobody lives full-time. Sometimes cars are parked there, but most of the time it's empty. She told me how to get there."

Zack twisted his torso around to look at Cupcake. They exchanged some kind of silent communication that made them both solemnly nod their heads.

Zack fingered the phone speaker attached to his ear and spoke quietly. "We're on the road to the house. Stand by."

Turning to me, Zack said, "Dixie, after we talked to you, Cupcake and the other guys agreed on what we'd do if we found out for sure that Opal was here in a house."

"What's your plan?"

"I'll explain it later. Let's drive on."

Everybody wanted to wait until later to tell me important things. I hate later.

I said, "You're not afraid we'll get stuck too?"

He shook his head. "Different tires, different weight, different driver."

We rolled on, straining to see ahead, our tires gnawing their way through the ruts Vern's limo had left. The road got more narrow and uneven, with deep holes dug by rain and time. We bumped along until we came to a side road with a rotting sign that gave a street name we couldn't read. There were no houses on the road. Evidently, the Empire Estates hadn't sold well. At another intersection, we drove to the end of yet another lurching sandy road. The car's motor hummed in concert with the whine of mosquitos rising from the surrounding palmettos and sawgrass.

After about a mile, the road made a right angle. Another

quarter mile, and Zack's forefinger pointed toward a copse of trees ahead. "A house is in there. Pull over."

I couldn't see it, and from Cupcake's silence I didn't think he could either. But a metal gate ran across a driveway that one could assume led to a house, so I pulled to the road's edge and parked. I could barely make out a chain running from a gatepost to the top of the gate, but I knew people rarely lock gate padlocks. Too much trouble for the owners to get out of their cars and unlock the things every time they go through, so the chains only serve as notice that the place is off-limits. If you drive in, you could be shot for trespassing. If you sneak in like we intended, you could be shot and displayed on a metal spike as a warning to others.

We sat panting like stressed dogs for a moment, then Zack pushed his door open and slid out of the car. I leaned to grab my 4-C-cell flashlight from the space between the front seats, touched the .38 at the back of my jeans to reassure myself it was still there, and got out too.

With flashlight and gun, those two "weapons of opportunity" that no cop is ever without, I felt as if I were back in uniform. Hit somebody on the head with a gun barrel, that's using a "weapon of opportunity." Hit them with the handle of a flashlight, that's another "weapon of opportunity." With the woods full of feral hogs and other swine, I figured I needed all the weapons of opportunity I could lay my hands on.

Cupcake got out last, squeezing his bulk through the opening like an enormous baby being born of a Bronco. We stood a moment beside a ditch that ran beside the road, getting our bearings and letting our feet get accustomed to the lay of the land before we moved forward. On the other side of the ditch, a swath of sawgrass lay silvered by wan moonlight. Beyond the sawgrass, a dark morass of trees and shrubs led to the spot where Zack thought he'd seen a house. As I looked across the ditch, I made out the dark outline of a vulture in a skeletal cypress tree. It may have been my imagination, but it seemed to me that the bird turned its head and looked at me.

Speaking low, Zack said, "When we get there, we'll go to the front door and engage whoever's inside while you go around to the back door. You'll go in and look for Opal. When you find her, you'll bring her out and get in the car. When we see you, we'll leave."

"That's your plan?"

He nodded solemnly, his head bobbing like a shadow puppet against the muzzy night. "The other guys will cover our backs."

I stifled a nervous giggle. He had left out so many moves that it was almost funny, except I knew very well what those moves were going to be, and it wasn't at all funny.

Cupcake leaned forward and spoke close to my ear. "If you want me to, I'll go inside with you. Just in case you need muscle."

That made me actually sputter a laugh that sounded like the bark of a teacup chihuahua puppy. Zack was a Boy Scout with a keen mind for electronics and motors and speed ratios and probably a lot of things I didn't know diddly about. Cupcake was a mountain with a sweet smile and dainty feet who could stop other mountains carrying footballs. But when it came to rescuing Opal, they were babes in the woods. In a few minutes I would be confronting hardened criminals, and all I had for backup were two innocent children.

I said, "I have my gun."

Zack said, "You won't need that."

Cupcake said, "Nah, we won't need no bullets."

From the tone of their voices I knew they were thinking I was a female on the verge of hysteria.

Zack pointed into the thick growth beside the road. "Okay."

Zack and Cupcake crossed the ditch and melted into the shadows under the trees, and I followed them. Cupcake led the way, his massive bulk pushing through palmetto fronds like the prow of a boat winding through mangroves. I walked in his footsteps, close enough to his broad back to avoid being hit by swishing fronds, and Zack brought up the rear, plodding stolidly through swarms of mosquitos and veils of spiderwebs. Every now and then one of us would catch a toe on an exposed root and stumble with whispered curses.

Above us, the tree canopy was so thick it blotted out every glint of night light. Below us, our shuffling feet stirred composted leaves that gave off a dank odor of mold and mildew mixed with animal urine. We moved through a timeless place that would have been cheerless even in bright sunshine. In the darkness, it seemed downright sepulchral.

After what I judged to be about the length of a football field, Cupcake stopped, held his left forearm out to the side, and waggled his fist. The movement must have been some sort of code for Zack, because he touched my shoulder and mimed for me to veer right and come up at the rear of the house.

This was apparently the moment when Zack and Cupcake expected me to slip into the house and grab Opal while they chatted up her kidnapper at the front door. It was a stupid plan, but for the moment it was the only plan we had.

Zack and Cupcake angled to the left and continued parallel to the road, while I tried to guide myself in a kind of arc that would take me to the back door of a house I still hadn't seen. I wasn't even positive Zack had seen it. For all I knew, all that lay ahead was more of what we were in.

Without Cupcake's back to shield me, I walked with one hand raised to touch tree trunks and hanging palm fronds before I stumbled into them. With every step, I prayed my booted toes didn't disturb a rattlesnake's sleep or catch the attention of a marauding wild hog. To my left, the trees along the road had thinned to a narrow strip, but I didn't see any sign of Zack or Cupcake.

After a century or two, I spotted a weak light glinting through a narrow gap in the curtain of trees. Cautiously, I navigated a shallow ditch and continued forward through undergrowth and low branches.

The dark rectangle of a tall house emerged in such sudden relief that it startled me. Like a lot of Florida real estate gone to seed, the house had probably been built as a summer getaway with living quarters upstairs and a screened "Florida room" downstairs. Its redwood siding was blackened by mildew and mold, and in the screened lower half, where somebody had once planned to hold neighborhood get-togethers, a few lawn chairs sat at awkward angles. Upstairs, a dull light shone through a small square of opaque glass—most likely a bathroom window—but I didn't see any movement behind it.

In its dark isolation, the house had the appearance of a melancholy memory of things best forgotten. As my eyes adjusted to its shape, I made out the outline of a compact sports car parked on a depressed graveled area to my left. It appeared to be red, probably a BMW. The last time I'd seen a car like that, it had been leaving Myra's house.

A twig cracked with the sound of a pistol shot. It could have been Zack or Cupcake who stepped on it. Or a look-out guarding the house readying his gun to empty into me. Or an owl peering down to see what fool thing a human was doing.

Around me, the night had gone silent, the way it does when an intruder causes nature to hold its breath. No tree frog chirps, no screech owl cries, not even whirrs of insect wings. As if it bore witness, the night waited for the house to divulge its secrets. Cautiously, I moved to the back of the BMW and dropped to my knees. From that angle, I could make out the rectangular frame of a door set in the screened lower half of the house.

A blurred silhouette moved behind the opaque glass of the upstairs window, and then the window went black. The shadow behind the glass was adult-sized, but it could have been male or female. In a minute heavy footsteps thudded down invisible stairs, and a man-shaped shadow moved through the gloom behind the screen. I had hoped it was Angelina, and a nasty taste of disappointment burned my throat when the door opened and an unmistakable man stepped out, furtively catching the screen door before it slapped shut. He was broad-shouldered, muscular, looked as if he could defend himself in a fight. He could have been Vern. Or he could have been one of the men with Vern when I was kidnapped. Or he could have been an innocent man who lived in this house and had no connection to Vern at all.

He walked a few feet away from the house and lit a cigarette. In the flare of the lighter I caught a momentary glimpse of his features. Not enough to identify him, but enough to see that he was Caucasian and clean-shaven. He smoked in concentrated drags, pulling on the cigarette as if he wanted to reduce its length in a hurry. I couldn't see any sign of a weapon, but that didn't mean he wasn't armed.

My heart pounded so loud I was afraid he would hear it. I wondered if Cupcake and Zack were watching the man too, or if they were at the front door of the house. As naïve as they'd seemed about the dangers in what we were doing, I could imagine them drawing straws to see who would knock.

A muffled wailing noise sounded from inside the house, and the man spun as if the noise frightened him. Flipping his cigarette to the ground, he jerked open the screen door and charged through, letting it slap shut with a sharp cracking sound. The man's dark outline melded with the blackness inside the screened enclosure, and in a minute the dull crying sound stopped as abruptly as it had started.

My mind ticked off all the possible sources of the oddly muted sound. It could have been a cat mewing. It could have been the sound of an electronic alarm of some kind. But I believed it had been a crying baby. I believed it had been Opal. Not Opal crying in a baby's normal cry, but in a way that had been strangely baffled. My mind backed away from images of all the possibilities for that dulled sound, along with reasons the crying had stopped so abruptly. I clung to the hope that Angelina was in the house, and that she had rushed to pick Opal up and give her a bottle. The chances of that being true seemed fewer every second.

The red BMW was an unexpected worry. Myra wasn't the only person in the world who drove that model, but its presence seemed too coincidental. Myra had left Sarasota in a car that looked like this one to bring Angelina to this house. If her car was here, that had to mean she was here as well. But why would Myra be upstairs in that unlit house with the man who had come downstairs?

A nagging voice in my head suggested that the BMW belonged to the man who had tossed away his cigarette when he heard his baby cry. His wife might be working in town while he watched their child, and Opal and Angelina might be miles away in another house.

# 28

omething wide loomed at my side and set my heart chuddering.

Cupcake's hoarse whisper cut through the darkness. "Is that you, Dixie?"

My own whisper sounded too much like a bobcat's hiss. "Yes! Where's Zack?"

"In front. A limo's hidden in the yard."

For a moment I felt elated at the presence of a limo, because it had to mean that Vern was in the house. Unless it was somebody else's limo. In the next moment, the futility of what we were doing suddenly came in waves. Our entire trip was insane. We were insane. We had strung together a theory based on a story told by a drunken braggart at a bar, then leaped to follow directions from a woman who might have been having fun with visiting yahoos, and set off into dark woods where we could get shot by a limo-driving homeowner who heard us blundering around his property.

So low my words were more exhaled than spoken, I said, "I'm not sure Opal is in there."

I could hear Cupcake's breathing. He probably used up as much oxygen in one breath as most people take in ten. When he spoke, it was in the same exhaled whisper I'd used. "We're not sure it's *not* her, either."

I couldn't argue with his logic, and for a moment I argued our case to an imaginary judge with a robotic voice. I admitted that even though any thinking person could have driven a fleet of trucks through the big holes in our evidence, we weren't entirely off the wall in thinking Opal was inside that house. We weren't hundred percent kooks, only maybe seventy-five percent. But as I told the imaginary judge, if everybody waited until they were positive before they took risks, no babies would ever get rescued.

The imaginary judge was not impressed. He reminded me that if my evidence was sound enough to justify my hiding in the darkness with a loaded gun stuck in the waistband of my jeans, it was sound enough to notify the local law enforcement office. The imaginary judge got specific. He suggested that I call Sergeant Owens and fill him in on all the information Zack, Cupcake, and I had collected. He stressed that Owens could then pass the evidence on to the FBI agents when they joined the case so that county, state, and federal agencies could team up and come streaming to our side.

The imaginary judge must have read too many action comic books or seen too many episodes of *CSI*, because his idea of how the law worked was laughably unrealistic. Following his advice would mean losing critical time trying to convince disbelieving law enforcement professionals that a leading citizen of vast wealth was behind the kidnapping of a baby, and that the baby was being held in a remote house outside a little town forty miles from the kidnap site. Even if we succeeded in convincing them, vital time would be lost while various agencies sparred over who had jurisdiction. After that was settled, a search warrant would have to be issued for an address we didn't have, something that could take several hours. And while we waited for the wheels of justice to make their agonizingly slow turns, the likelihood was high that word would leak to Kantor Tucker. If that happened, Opal would be disposed of before anybody went looking for her.

We had no choice but to save her. Furthermore, Zack's idea of going to the front door and distracting the kidnapper while I went in the back and got Opal no longer seemed so squirrelly.

Hunkered beside me, Cupcake seemed to realize I'd come to a decision. "Now?"

I took a deep breath and nodded. "Let's do it."

I'm not sure what I expected him to do, but it wasn't what he did. Still squatting on his heels, he lifted his head and whistled. Not a referee kind of whistle, but a long, quivering, mournful trill like a screech owl makes, starting low, rising to a tremulous wail, and abruptly ending. An answering cry came from the darkness at the front of the house. Hearing one screech owl's eerie cry in the dark woods is enough to make rational people look over their shoulders for ghosts. Hearing two raises the hairs on the back of your neck.

Cupcake grinned, his white teeth flashing like the Cheshire cat's smile.

In the next instant, a loud pounding cut through the darkness, a sound like a heavy stick hammering against a front door.

At the same time, a man's drunken voice yelled, "Hey, Clyde! Open up! It's me, Leon! Clyde? I know you're in there! Open up! Hoo-ya! Hey, Clyde! You hear me, Clyde?"

It took a minute for me to realize the drunk at the front door was Zack.

The house remained dark and silent.

The pounding got louder and Zack's voice raised to a sharp-edged roar that half the county could probably hear. "Come on, Clyde! I got women coming! Open the door! Women are behind me, good-looking women! They wanta meet you, you old dog! It's Leon, dude! We gonna party! We gonna party hardy! Woo-ha!"

Cupcake touched my shoulder. "Let's roll."

For such a large man, Cupcake moved across the sandy yard with surprising speed. With me behind his elbow, he went through the screened door and moved directly to the wall-hugging stairway to the upper floor. With my flashlight's barrel resting on my shoulder, I gripped it by the bulb end and followed Cupcake to the second level.

The open doorway to the second-floor living space made a black rectangle against a dark gray interior. Cupcake took one side of the opening and I took the other, both of us angling our heads into the space to look into a large open room. Windows were open for ventilation, but what little air drifted in was heavy and humid.

A man stood at a window facing the road. The window had venetian blinds and the man had pulled one slat up to peer through. Downstairs at the front door, Zack continued to make a loud racket. In the night's stillness, the noise could be heard for miles. The man apparently knew that, because his entire body jittered with increasing nervousness.

Cupcake eased his bulk around the door facing and flattened himself against the wall. I followed his lead, pressing my back against the wall beside the door. So the whites of my eyes wouldn't give me away, I tilted my head back and lowered my eyelids to look through thin slits. I was afraid Cupcake wouldn't know to do that, but he had the same chin-up profile. Probably learned in Indian Guides or Boy Scouts how to slip through darkness. He must have also learned how to sneak up on a man listening to a drunk's yelling, because he melted into the shadows and moved toward the front window.

I heard no baby sounds, smelled no baby scents. Their absence was alarming. Perhaps the cry I'd heard earlier hadn't been Opal after all. Or perhaps it had been and she had been permanently silenced.

Thrashing, clattering, grunting sounds at the front window told me that Cupcake had reached the man and taken him by surprise. I couldn't see the fight, but I recognized the sickening sound of fists hitting bare skin, and the hoarse choking sound of somebody's breath cut off by a squeezing hand or by the edge of a stiffened palm hitting a hyoid bone. Cupcake was bigger, but the other man was obviously familiar with dirty fighting. Downstairs, where Zack couldn't hear the fight, the yelling and pounding continued.

I had to have light to find Opal. With my big flashlight still resting on my shoulder so it pointed down, I thumbed the switch to make a wide circle of light. The room's dark periphery where Cupcake and the man fought was now a lighter shade of black.

I moved the light along the wall to my right, where a double bed with a mussed yellow chenille bedspread was shoved against the wall. In the center of the room was a sagging sofa, a reclining chair with white stuffing spilling through cracks in the fake leather upholstery, a card table, and some folding chairs. No crib, no playpen, no sign of a baby.

In the far corner beyond the bed, an apartment-sized range and refrigerator made a kitchen area, along with an abbreviated countertop with a sink. A gathered plastic skirt hid the pipes under the sink. A door was ajar at the edge of the kitchen area. I imagined the door led to a bathroom, but I'd have to pass through the fighting men to get to it. Sweeping my light slowly around the room to illumine every inch, I scanned the room with mounting panic. When I moved the light across the spot where Cupcake and the man continued to thrash and grunt, I saw two straight chairs pushed against the wall behind them. Myra Kreigle was in one, Angelina in the other. Both women were bound and gagged, with duct tape over their mouths like Vern and his goons had put over mine. Myra's eyes were furious and demanding. Angelina's were terrified and pleading.

I had to make a decision, and I had to make it fast. The women's presence meant the plans Myra and Tucker had made had gone terribly wrong. The man fighting Cupcake was stuck with Myra as a hostage and Angelina as a witness to a host of crimes. If Vern's buddies were outside watching Zack, they knew Cupcake and I were inside, and any second might find them up the stairs and holding guns on us. We could end up as trussed and helpless as Myra and Angelina.

To get to the bathroom door and look behind it, I'd have to pass through the fight. To get to Angelina and set her free—setting Myra free was not an option—I'd also have to pass through the fight.

In the nanosecond that I weighed choices, my light caught Cupcake's eyes and caused him to stumble backward against the venetian blinds. In the bright light, his nose streamed blood, and his eyes had the astonished look of a Goliath realizing that a smaller man might best him. Taking advantage of Cupcake's momentary loss of balance, the other man's hand dipped toward his ankle in a move that made me spring forward. My flashlight's handle made a satisfying crack on the back of his head, and he sagged to his knees.

Cupcake surged upright and gave me a dimpled grin. "You got some jiggy moves, girl."

I pulled my .38 from the back of my jeans and pointed it at the man's head.

It was Vern. He recognized me at the same time I recognized him.

Dazed, he sputtered, "Who? Wha . . . ?"

I said, "Cupcake, he has a gun in an ankle holster. Get it. He may have a knife too, so pat him down."

The look Cupcake gave me was probably the look a man in a bar gets when he realizes the woman he's been flirting with is his sister in a wig.

Vern was even more confused. "Who the hell are you?"

I said, "Long story, Vern. Where's the baby?"

His swelling eyes took on a sly look. "What baby?"

I spun away from him and pushed open the door to a miniscule bathroom. No tub, just a metal shower enclosure. No baby inside it.

Zack had stopped yelling, which either meant he had seen the light behind the blinds or that somebody had grabbed him and silenced him.

I ran to Angelina and grabbed an end of tape covering her mouth. I said, "Sorry, but I have to do this."

Tears sprang to her eyes when I ripped the tape off her lips. I knew exactly how she felt.

I said, "Where's the baby?"

She began to weep in earnest. "I do not know! I hear baby cry, but is dark and I do not see!"

Behind the tape on her mouth, Myra made a guttural sound of demand and jerked her head and shoulders side to side.

I said, "Cupcake, you got a knife?"

He grunted and moved to Angelina's chair. While he cut through the tape holding her hands and feet, I turned back to Vern. He was getting his wits back, no longer swaying with dizziness.

I put the barrel of my revolver against his temple. "Here's the deal, Vern. As far as I'm concerned, men who harm babies should be strung up by their gonads and left to turn slowly in the wind. I could do that. Or I could kill you and save somebody else the trouble. If I kill you, the cops will pin it on the guy you left here today with the baby. They'll think he waited until you came back and then he shot you in the head. So if you have any interest in staying alive, tell me where the baby is, and I'll think about letting you keep breathing."

The thing about making threats to low-life people is that they only believe you if you really mean what you say. At that moment, I meant every word. I don't know if I would have carried out the threat, but when I said it I thought I would. I wanted to do Vern serious harm, and he knew it.

He licked his lips. He shifted his eyes back and forth. His Adam's apple bobbled.

He said, "Under the bed."

Behind him, Cupcake was helping Angelina stand, and she was stamping her feet to get life back into them. Myra squealed with fury and flashed her dark eyes. The bitch expected us to rescue her, set her free, have compassion for her. Tough titty.

I ran to the bed, dropped to the floor, and raised the ratty chenille bedspread to peer under it. All I saw among the dust bunnies and dead spiders was a small cedar chest, the kind southern women store their woolen sweaters in. With my heart pounding, I dragged the box out and opened it.

Surrounded by a putrid odor of old urine, Opal lay atop a skimpy bed of rumpled T-shirts. Her eyes were closed and her breath was so shallow I was afraid at first that she was dead. Tenderly, I scooped her up and clutched her to my chest. Then I stood up and ran down the stairs and outside. I was almost to the front of the house when I heard Cupcake's thundering footsteps and Angelina's whimpers behind me.

Zack materialized out of the gloom, his pale face grim and rigid.

I said, "I have Opal!" I didn't add that she was sleeping with a stillness that could only come from drugs.

He said, "Come on!" If he noticed Angelina, he didn't say anything.

With Angelina's soft cries and Cupcake's heaving breath behind us, we raced across the sandy yard, floundered across the ditch, and thrashed through weeds like rogue elephants on a rampage. At the road, we ran like hell. Or at least Zack and I did. Angelina was slow and Cupcake hung back to steady her. Halfway to the Bronco, he flung Angelina over his shoulder like a sack of flour.

A crack of rifle fire sounded behind us. I hollered, "Fan out! Serpentine!"

Zack said, "What?"

Cupcake wheezed, "Zigzag!"

As we reached the Bronco, I heard a car engine start. I was sure Vern didn't intend to chase us in his heavy limo, but Myra's car was light and available.

Zack yelled, "I'll drive!"

No argument from me. I said, "Keys are in the ignition!"

Setting Angelina on her feet and slinging open the back door so she could crawl inside, Cupcake wrenched open the front passenger door, helped me maneuver in with Opal in my arms, then flung himself in the back. Angelina's face was wet with tears, but she looked relieved.

Zack started the engine and moved the car slowly forward. Headlights flashed behind us. Zack turned on our own lights and goosed the Bronco through the sand as fast as he dared. More rifle shots sounded.

Cupcake said, "I sure hope he's a bad shot."

I said, "If he hits us it'll be pure dumb luck. But it might be a good idea for you and Angelina to hunker down so your heads aren't sticking up."

Zack said, "You do that too. You and Opal."

I slid to the edge of the seat so I wasn't such a good target. Nobody spoke the fact that Zack's head was sticking up in clear outline. Preoccupied with driving and muttering instructions to his friends on the highway, he probably didn't even think about it.

# 29

We made it down the bumpy sand road to Gator Trail without being shot. Vern drove too fast and too erratically to get off a hit. He even managed to get stuck for a minute in the same furrows he'd made with his limo. Vern was a perfect example of a man who never learned from his past mistakes.

Zack drove carefully until we turned onto Gator Trail, and then it seemed to me that we were going faster than my Bronco was meant to go. But Zack held the wheel with such a sure touch that I decided we must not be going as fast as I thought. Then I looked at the speedometer and realized we were going even faster. Cars must recognize the touch of an expert driver and pull out all their reserves.

Vern slewed onto Gator Trail behind us, and fired off another couple of shots. The idiot must have thought he was in a movie. At the juncture with State Road 72, Zack slowed to let Vern get closer, and then at the last moment cut the Bronco hard to the left. As he did, a line of clunker cars appeared out of the darkness to form an L-shaped barrier that forced Vern to make a sharp turn to the right.

Tires screamed. Metal screeched. The BMW slewed, slammed broadside into the railing over Horse Creek, lifted on one side for a moment, and then rolled over the railing.

I said, "Vern went into the water."

Zack said, "Too bad."

Cupcake sighed. "Pull over, man."

Zack grimaced, but he edged the car to the side of the road and stopped. Cupcake hauled himself out of the backseat, hiked back to the bridge, and disappeared down the embankment toward the water. Angelina whimpered under her breath. I imagined she feared that Cupcake would bring Vern back to ride with us, but I didn't have the energy to reassure her. The other drivers had gathered on the bridge to look over the broken railing. The men on the bridge were silent.

While we waited, I pulled my cellphone from my jeans pocket and dialed Sergeant Owens. When he answered, I spoke tersely.

"I'm in DeSoto County with Zack Carlyle. We have his kidnapped baby. We found her in a house where Vern Brogher was holding her. He also had Myra Kreigle and another woman bound and gagged in chairs. We left Myra in the house. The other woman is with us. She's a witness to several crimes. Vern Brogher has had an accident in which his car rolled into Horse Creek. Cupcake Trillin has gone into the river to rescue him. Zack and I are going to take the baby to her mother at the Charter Hotel on Midnight Pass Road. I'd appreciate it if you'd have a physician meet us there and examine the baby. She seems healthy, but I think she's been drugged."

Several beats went by.

Sergeant Owens said, "Horse Creek. Charter Hotel. I'll get on it right away." Owens has never been what you'd call an effusive man.

I ended the call and shoved the phone back into my pocket. I patted Opal on the back. I hummed a little tune close to her ear. Her breath was warm on my neck.

The Bronco's engine rumbled under the hood as if it objected to sitting still. Zack looked as if he had the same objection. After several minutes, one of the men on the bridge trotted to us and leaned through Zack's window.

"Cupcake fished the son of a bitch out. He's alive. Cupcake's holding him until the cops come. We'll wait for them. You go on."

Zack said, "Thanks, man. For everything."

He revved the engine and pulled back to the highway.

For some reason known only to babies, Opal chose that moment to wake up. Still groggy from whatever Vern had given her, she pulled her head back from my chest and gave me a goofy grin.

Softly, I said, "Hey, Opal."

As if she understood that she was out of danger, she gurgled a half-laugh.

Zack turned his head and stared at her as if the sound shocked him. Then he laughed too, a rollicking sound of pure joy.

# 30

Halfway back to Sarasota, we met several speeding green-and-whites from the sheriff's department. Their sirens were blaring, and I knew they hoped to get to Horse Creek before deputies from DeSoto County arrived there. A little farther on, we met TV vans with uplink dishes sprouting from their roofs like mushrooms. The reporters inside were probably salivating like bloodhounds at the idea of filming the arrest of the man who had kidnapped a famous race car driver's baby, only to be saved from drowning by a famous inside linebacker for the Bucs. I still didn't know what an inside linebacker was, but Cupcake was a man I was proud to know.

Opal drifted back to sleep, waking every few minutes with more alert awareness. She smelled to high heaven, and she was so wet that she'd soaked through my sweatshirt. When we got to Sarasota's outskirts, I pointed to a strip center where a 7-Eleven was open.

"We need to get diapers for Opal."

Zack looked surprised, as if the idea of diapers was

alien to him, but he pulled into the lot and cut the engine.

I said, "Get the Size Two kind. I think they'll fit. And get a box of wet wipes too."

"You want *me* to get them?"

"Yeah, Zack. You're her father."

A smile flitted across his face. "How about baby food? Should I get something for her to eat?"

"Good idea. Maybe some strained fruit. We can go for other stuff later."

From the backseat, Angelina said, "I get it."

She had her hand on the door handle, ready to jump out. I pushed the child-lock gizmo on my door to make it impossible for the back door to open.

I said, "Zack, hurry."

He must have understood that Angelina intended to run away, because he slid out of the car, slammed the door closed, and went into the 7-Eleven at a fast clip.

I said, "Sorry, Angelina, but you have to stay with us. You must talk to the police, tell them everything you know."

Wide-eyed with fear, she said, "Mr. Tucker will kill my mother."

"Mr. Tucker is going to jail, Angelina. He won't hurt you or your mother. But you have to tell what you know about him and about Myra Kreigle."

"That man at the house."

"Him too. The man's name is Vern. They're all going to jail, Angelina."

She didn't trust a word I said, and continued to push against the door as if sheer force would make it open.

Inside the 7-Eleven, Zack was talking to the cashier and gesturing toward the car. The cashier looked through the glass at us, then hurried from behind the counter and led Zack behind an aisle. In a moment they hurried out, both of them carrying items in their arms. From the enthusiasm of the cashier, I figured he must have known who Zack was. I was sure of it when I saw Zack hand him cash and then write something on a slip of paper. I guess famous people can't even buy diapers without leaving autographs.

Back in the car, Zack looked quickly at Angelina, then handed me a package of diapers and a plastic bag holding a clutter of baby food jars and a box of baby wipes. As he backed the car from the parking place, Angelina moaned with despair.

By the time I got Opal cleaned and changed, my nose was wrinkled and Zack looked as if he might barf at the odor.

After I stuffed the soiled diaper in the plastic grocery bag, he said, "Holy shit!"

I laughed. "Just normal baby shit, Zack. Find an open Dumpster and I'll throw it away."

"Do they all smell like that?"

"Just when they haven't been changed for twelve hours. Opal always smells sweet and clean. She has a good mother."

"You think I'm a real horse's ass, don't you?"

"I don't know what kind of ass you are. All I know is that a baby needs both parents."

"Ruby left me. She took our baby and left."

I couldn't argue with that.

I said, "I'm just guessing here, but did your father have anything to do with her leaving?"

He took so long to answer that even Angelina stopped whimpering to hear what he had to say.

"Dad never trusted her."

"How many women would you say your dad *does* trust?"

He took even longer to answer that. "I can't think of any."

"Zack, was your mom a good woman?"

"She never said a mean thing about any human being. Never did a mean thing in her life."

"But your dad didn't trust her."

He sighed. "Okay."

We rode silently down Clark Road, crossed Tamiami Trail where Clark Road becomes Stickney Point Road, and rolled over the drawbridge to Siesta Key. At Midnight Pass Road, Zack turned toward the Charter Hotel. I wanted to ask him what he planned to do about Ruby, but I kept quiet. Opal was wide awake now, lying on my lap looking around with eyes so dark blue they were almost violet.

Zack said, "My mom's eyes were like Opal's."

I didn't remind him that he had the same eyes. It was possible that he'd always been so focused on electronics and speed that he'd never taken a good look at himself in the mirror.

When we pulled into the Charter Hotel parking lot, we saw several sheriff's cars, an ambulance, and a few ubiquitous panel trucks from TV stations. Angelina moaned again. She apparently thought all the attention was for herself.

Zack pulled under the hotel portico, where a uniformed bellman stepped forward. "Sorry, sir. You can't park here. We're expecting somebody the police are meeting."

Zack's eyes narrowed. "I believe we're the somebody. Tell the cops to keep the reporters away while we get out of the car."

"I can't park it for you, sir. We don't have the insurance to cover valet parking."

It was such an inane non sequitur that Zack tilted his head back to look under his eyelids at the man. "Maybe you can get one of the cops to park it."

As he spoke, a uniformed deputy tapped on my window, and I turned my head to see Deputy Jesse Morgan peering in at me. Morgan is the Key's only sworn deputy. He and I have had occasion to meet over dead bodies enough times for him to believe that I have a dark cloud over my head. I was happy that this time was different.

I lowered my window, smiled at him, and tilted my chin toward Opal.

He said, "Ms. Hemingway," but he looked past me at Zack. From the excited gleam in his eyes, I almost expected him to ask for an autograph like the 7-Eleven guy.

I said, "Officer Morgan, this is the baby that was kidnapped this morning. We're taking her to her mother here in the hotel, and we'd appreciate it if you'd keep the reporters away from us."

"We'll do our best, but you know how it goes."

I knew that journalists were allowed anywhere in the public viewpoint, as a sidewalk or street or right of way, and they could take photos from any of those places. A business or a hotel open to the public is considered a public place, but hotel lobbies and hallways are gray areas, sometimes considered private and sometimes public, depending on the nature of the crime committed there. Since most journalists operate under the philosophy that it's better to be chased away than to be denied permission, I expected a volley of shouted questions to surround us when we left the car.

I said, "The woman in the backseat is a witness to several crimes. She is also a flight risk. She's frightened, and with good reason."

Morgan leaned down to look at Angelina. "Yes, ma'am."

He straightened and beckoned to a cluster of deputies at the edge of the portico. They trotted over, Morgan gave them quick orders, and when I released the child-lock control, they opened the back door and took Angelina into custody. They were gentle, but very firm. As they led her away, she looked over her shoulder at me with anguished reproach. Clearly, she didn't trust me any more than she trusted Myra.

The waiting journalists had only given the Bronco a passing glance. They must have expected Zack to arrive alone, zooming in like Batman with his baby on his back. They clearly hadn't expected a dusty SUV with a man and woman in the front and another woman in the back. But when a covey of journalists saw uniformed officers lead Angelina to a sheriff's car, they turned toward us like vultures sniffing carrion.

At the same moment, through the glass wall of the hotel lobby, I saw Ruby burst from one of the elevators. Her arms were already outstretched to hold her baby. I knew if she came outside she would be surrounded by a cacophony of bright lights, shoving reporters, and shouted questions. Zack saw her too, and had the same reaction as I did.

Simultaneously, we opened our car doors and ran toward the hotel entrance. Startled by the movement, Opal began to shriek, and I pulled her close to shield her from the lights and noise. We loped across the marbled lobby and met Ruby in the middle.

She was luminous and wild. I think if anybody had tried to stop her, she would have torn them to bits with her hands. I put Opal into her arms and Zack rushed to put his arm around them both. Behind us, Morgan and some other deputies arranged themselves in a meager phalanx in front of the entrance doors.

With Zack half-pushing, half-pulling Ruby, we ran across the lobby to the bank of elevators.

As we stepped into the elevator, I heard Morgan shout to the reporters. "Get a grip, people! You are not allowed to follow anybody to their hotel room. You are not allowed to wait outside their hotel room. If you want to camp out here in the parking lot, that's your business, but if any one of you tries to infringe on a hotel guest's rights, you'll be arrested."

I was impressed. I'd never seen Morgan so decisive.

Opal was still howling, and Ruby was crying while she tried to examine her for bruises or cuts.

I said, "She doesn't seem to be hurt."

Ruby wailed, "Why is she so *filthy*?"

Zack and I exchanged a look, remembering how much filthier she had been before we got clean diapers for her.

I said, "Did the sheriff's office send a physician?"

"He's in the suite with Granddad."

Zack stiffened. "Your grandfather's with you?"

She shot him a hostile glare. "He's an old man, Zack. His house almost burned to the ground this morning. Where else would he be?"

Zack seemed about to make a snappy retort, then crimped his lips into a straight line. I had the feeling they had argued about Ruby's grandfather and Zack's father so many times they had a repertoire of one-liners they could spit out on cue. I wished Cupcake were there to sweeten their practiced sourness.

When we got out at Ruby's floor, I saw Mr. Stern standing in the hall like a sentinel. Zack's jaw hardened when he saw him, the look of a young warrior preparing himself for battle against an older, more seasoned combatant.

But instead of taking a snarky attitude, Mr. Stern held his hand out to Zack. His eyes were fierce, but not with anger. As if she recognized him, Opal's cries subsided to droning hiccups.

Mr. Stern said, "Young man, let me be the first to tell you how much I admire what you did. That took guts. Real guts like most men your age don't have anymore. It's a privilege to shake your hand."

Abashed, Zack said, "Thank you, sir. But I didn't do it alone."

"A good offense takes teamwork, son! And only leaders who've proven themselves get smooth cooperation from their troops. It speaks well of you that you had people willing to help you."

Ruby and I rounded our eyes at each other. Mr. Stern had either undergone a profound change, or he'd been locked up and some other old man was impersonating him.

A chubby man in a sweatshirt with a stethoscope dangling from his neck came to the door.

"Bring the baby inside, please."

Ruby tightened her grip on Opal. "She seems fine. I think she just needs a bath."

"You can bathe her as soon as I check her."

We all trooped into the hotel suite and watched as the doctor took Opal and laid her on the bed. She began to cry, and so did Ruby.

The doctor removed Opal's grimy clothes, listened to her heart, looked into her nose and ears, examined her bottom, searched for bruises or scratches on her arms and legs, palpated her tummy, ran his hand over her skull, and pronounced her undamaged.

As Ruby snatched her and held her close, the doctor said, "How long has she gone without nourishment?"

We all looked at each other and shrugged. Only Vern or Angelina or Myra would know the answer to that, but we doubted she had been fed.

Zack said, "We can pick up whatever she needs on the way home."

Over Opal's head, Ruby looked a question at him.

A crimson flush climbed Zack's pale neck and crept to his hairline. "We'll all be going home *where we belong*." I wondered if he had picked up the line from Cupcake.

Turning to Mr. Stern, he said, "We can pick up your cat from the hospital, too."

For a second, Mr. Stern's entire face smiled. Then he looked at Ruby and Opal, and grew sober. "You young people need some time alone. Away from old men and cats and everybody else." He flashed a look at me, and I felt my own face heat.

I said, "Until you can move back into your own home, I think we can find a hotel that will allow you and Cheddar to share a room."

"Tomorrow," he said. "This day's had enough."

So had we all.

In a quick flurry of hugs and handshakes, Ruby and Zack hurried out to the hallway. I stayed a second to tell Mr. Stern that I would find him a new hotel the next morning, and then followed them. We were all dragging with fatigue and relief.

On the way to Zack's house, we stopped at a Walmart where Ruby ran in to scoop up everything she could find that Opal might ever conceivably need. Zack and I sat in the car with Opal and waited. Opal was fussy, every minute more wide awake from whatever Vern had used to drug her—the doctor had guessed paregoric. Part of me was furious that she'd been drugged, another part was grateful. I hoped her trauma had been lessened by being asleep for most of her ordeal.

Before Ruby returned to us, Zack made several phone calls, the first to Cupcake.

"Opal's okay, bro." A pause, then, "I'm taking them home right now. Ruby's in the Walmart buying stuff for the baby, then we'll go home." Another pause, and a husky, "Thanks for everything, buddy."

As he dialed the next number, he glanced at me. "Cupcake says the cops took Vern to jail. Also Myra."

Before I could answer, his phone connection clicked.

"Dad, it's me. I'm on my way home with Ruby and our baby. I'd like you to be gone when we get there."

I heard gruff squawking sounds, and Zack sighed.

"Go home where you belong, Dad. Stay in your own house, not mine. I'm bringing my family home and we're going to stay there together, the three of us. If you disrespect my wishes on this, you won't see me again. Ever."

He looked out his window and saw Ruby tearing across the parking lot with several large shopping bags hanging from her arms and shoulders.

He said, "I have to give my wife a hand now, Dad. Goodbye."

In a flash, he was out of the car and helping stow bags into the backseat. Before Ruby climbed into the passenger seat beside me, he leaned down like a skinny comma and kissed her cheek. Ruby was trembling so much when she got in that she fumbled getting the seat belt to latch. I handed Opal to her and drove off smiling. One of the nicest surprises about life is that sometimes impossible things happen.

# 31

Zack, Cupcake, and I sat in the back row of the court-room during Ruby's swearing-in. Opal slept on Zack's shoulder, and he made sure that Ruby had a clear view of their daughter from the witness stand.

The bailiff held out a Bible for Ruby to place her left hand on, told her to raise her right hand, and asked the question we've all heard a million times on TV shows. "Do you swear to tell the truth, the whole truth, and nothing but the truth, so help you God?"

Standing straight and steady, Ruby swept her gaze over Myra and her team of defense attorneys, and then gave a tremulous smile to Zack. "I do."

The jig was up for Myra, and she knew it. Myra occupied a straight-backed wooden chair at the defendant's table. The chair looked uncomfortable. Myra looked cadaverous, pasty white and hollow-eyed.

Denied bond, Tuck was in jail and would be tried separately for his part in her Ponzi operation. After Ruby's testimony, he would spend as many years in prison as Myra.

Vern hadn't had anything to do with their Ponzi scheme, but he was in jail charged with kidnapping, illegal imprisonment, attempted murder, and an assortment of lesser crimes. He had been denied bond, and he would be in prison for a long time. To Mr. Stern's delight, one of the most damning pieces of evidence against Vern had been the presence of orange cat hairs on Vern's limo seat. DNA testing found the orange hairs had come from Cheddar, proof that Vern had picked up cat hairs when he lifted Opal from the crib where Cheddar had been allowed to visit while Ruby was in the room.

I didn't stay for Ruby's entire testimony. I had cats to groom and feed, and anyway the testimony would be dry and boring once it moved to the minutiae of money transfers and contracts and taxes and foreign bank accounts. Boring to me, anyway. Tom Hale would have found it juicy and riveting.

Mr. Stern and Cheddar were happily together at the Bide-A-Tide Villas on Turtle Beach. Cheddar had a screened lanai to watch shorebirds leaving tracks in the sand, and Mr. Stern had a row of history books about Florida that excited him as much as the birds excited Cheddar. Workmen were busy at Mr. Stern's house putting in new wallboard and floors in Ruby's bedroom, painting, replacing furniture, and getting rid of the odor of smoke throughout the house. I stopped by the Bide-A-Tide twice a day to give him a hand with Cheddar, and I went to the house once a day to feed the koi. Without Mr. Stern and Cheddar to give it life, the courtyard seemed strangely empty.

Sometimes when I was tossing fish food on the pond

for the koi, I had an eerie feeling that eyes were looking down at me from Myra's house, but the house was empty. Angelina had been questioned at length, and her answers had helped law enforcement officers connect the dots in several cases against Kantor Tucker. Like flying a man who was in the country illegally over the Gulf and shoving him out. The man could not be reported missing because he didn't legally exist, but Angelina knew his widow, and the widow could give dates and times that corresponded to a body that had washed up on Anna Maria Island.

As for me, I was in purgatory. Or hell. Or some weird place between lives like the Tibetan *bardo*.

People who aren't true to themselves are lost to everybody else as well. An easy thing to know, but a hard thing to do. In my imagination, I tried to place myself in a city where I breathed the odor of chicory coffee and beignets instead of sea air. I tried to imagine what it would be like to live in a place where jazz was the subliminal background sound instead of the sigh of surf and cries of seagulls.

All that was easy. It was even easy to imagine myself feeling joy in seeing Guidry's city through his eyes, getting to know his family, creating a home for us. The only problem was, I couldn't imagine doing it forever. A few weeks, maybe. A month or two. But I knew as sure as I knew the back of my own hand that I would wake up one morning and *need* the sounds and smells I'd known all my life. I would need them the same way I needed air. Without them, my soul would shrivel.

My mind desperately raced looking for compromise.

But I always ran up against the hard wall of knowing that compromise isn't possible when it comes to *needs*—the unique basics essential to a person's happiness. Needs can't be bartered or denied without something intrinsic to the soul dying. *Wants,* on the other hand, are just the things that make life more pleasant. They're like gravy on your mashed potatoes. Not essential, but nice to have. They can be compromised all over the place, but only after your basic needs are met.

And the hard truth is that while someone who loved me could give me some of my *wants,* the only person who could meet my *needs* was me.

The trick was to tell the difference between needs and wants.

When the levees holding back the sea outside New Orleans broke, the city suffered devastation unlike any this country has ever experienced. When artists, musicians, writers, culinary wizards, and ordinary citizens were driven away by the floods, New Orleans lost part of its soul. For Guidry, the urge to go home and be a part of recovering the city's soul was a *need,* not simply something that would add to his enjoyment of life. That need was something only he could define, and only he could meet. Loving him meant that I wouldn't try to stand in his way.

Myra Kreigle and her sort had caused financial ruin for a lot of hardworking people on Siesta Key, but I couldn't honestly say that I felt the Key needed me for its survival. With me or without me, Siesta Key would continue to be a beautiful place where gentle people walked the beach every morning, where they marked turtle and plover nests to keep them safe, where they rescued wounded manatees and seabirds.

The truth was that I needed the Key a lot more than it needed me. I needed its sand beneath my feet, needed to breathe its sea air, needed to hear the cries of seabirds and share space with tropical vegetation. Without them, I would not be me.

The truth was that while I greatly *wanted* Guidry's touch, his keen intellect, his loyalty, and his love, I would continue to be myself without them.

It was that truth that broke my heart.